THE THEFT of the VIRGIN

THE THEFT of the VIRGIN

by

JOHN SCHERBER

Replace that frame and you'll make it a
masterpiece.
—Bernard Berenson

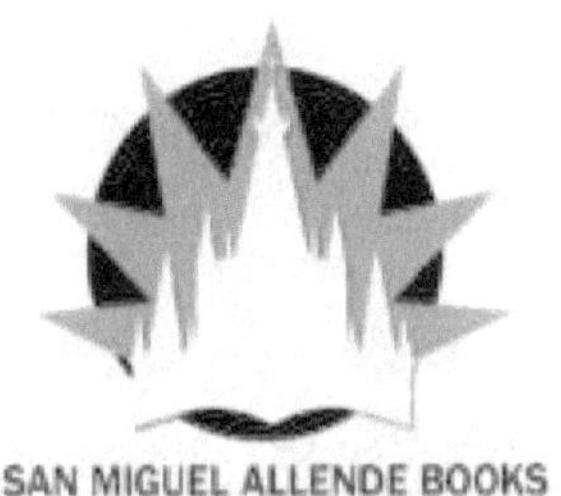

San Miguel Allende Books
San Miguel de Allende, GTO, México

ACKNOWLEDGEMENTS

Any book starts as an idea, and by its completion becomes a joint effort.

Thanks to my wife, Kristine, for editorial and critical help.

Thanks to my readers: Marilyn Krichman, Donna Krueger and Wendy Weber

Cover Design by Lander Rodriguez
Web Page Design by Julio Mendez

ISBN: 978-0-9832582-7-8

San Miguel Allende Books
San Miguel de Allende, GTO, México
www.sanmiguelallendebooks.com

Also by John Scherber

NONFICTION

San Miguel de Allende: A Place in the Heart
A Writer's Notebook
Into the Heart of Mexico
Living in San Miguel

FICTION

The Devil's Workshop
Eden Lost
The Amarna Heresy
Beyond Terrorism: Survival

(The Murder in Mexico series)

Twenty Centavos
The Fifth Codex
Brushwork
Daddy's Girl
Strike Zone
Vanishing Act
Jack and Jill
Identity Crisis
The Book Doctor
The Predator
The Girl from Veracruz
Angel Face
Uneasy Rider
Lost in Chiapas

(The Townshend Vampire Trilogy)

And Dark My Desire

And Darker My Wrath

For Kristine

PROLOGUE
PIET VERGRUEN AND HIS COLLECTION
LONDON, MAY, 1938

James Carruthers, the appraiser recommended by Sotheby's, made a final pass by the eight paintings, pausing for two or three minutes before each. His expression was unreadable. Piet Vergruen, the owner, waited without anxiety. He thought he already knew their value. Before this meeting, he had made a list with his best estimate, but he needed a written appraisal for new insurance coverage in England. Outside the Thames warehouse, the morning fog clung to the windows just below the roof.

"I am going to estimate them at £140,000 in total," Carruthers said at last. "You'll have it in writing by the end of the week."

Vergruen was expecting twice this amount.

"So the market in old masters is severely depressed here?"

"I wouldn't say that, but it's not enthusiastic either."

"But why so little?"

"You have a problem with three of them. The Rembrandt and the two Franz Hals. All three are forgeries."

Vergruen took a step away from the appraiser.

"But how can you say that? They've been in my family for years."

"Well, for one thing, this Rembrandt has also been in a private collection in France for more than 200 years. I've seen it. For another, both the Franz Hals paintings have the look of Han van Meegeren, one of the world's best forgers. Many think he's the equal of Hals. Don't take it too hard, he's deceived the best collectors in the world."

"*Is* the equal of Hals?"

"Yes, van Meegeren is still alive, but no one knows where he is."

Vergruen turned and stared at the brick wall of the bonded warehouse at the edge of the river. "These paintings were all purchased by my father," he said after a while, stroking his goatee.

"Then you have no reason to reproach yourself. Do you know what he paid for them?"

"He would never discuss that with me."

"Today, these three forgeries would bring perhaps £500 total at auction, correctly labeled, of course. My appraisal will properly identify them, so I don't think your insurer would even offer coverage. I'm sorry, but this happens. I'm just the messenger." He gave Vergruen an ironic smile.

They left together, the guards locking up behind them. As he got into the waiting taxi, Vergruen had already decided what he would do with the three forgeries.

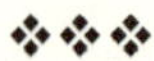

Piet Vergruen was a third-generation Dutch

chocolatier who had become increasingly uncomfortable with the political developments in Europe in the thirties. After the Nazi takeover of Czechoslovakia, and then soon after, of Austria, he sold his factory to a German whose family had lived in the Hague for many years, and moved with his wife, two daughters, and his recipes to England, where he made a new start. He had signed a non-compete agreement with the buyer that covered the Continent, but England was wide open to him.

In addition to numerous pictures of lesser value, he brought with him the collection of eight old masters from his father's estate that included the three fakes. It was good that Vergruen didn't need the money, but he didn't need the shock of the appraisal, either.

The shock proved to be short-lived, and when he retired in 1960 at the age of sixty-nine, he sold his English business to Cadbury, and with a portion of the proceeds, started a foundation to propagate information about forged artworks. He had also intentionally acquired numerous other forgeries over the years following the shocking appraisal, and exhibited them throughout Great Britain with seminars about forgery detection that proved popular with university faculty and students, and the general public. He loved to tour the shows anonymously himself, observing people's reactions. When he died in 1977, he left the bulk of his fortune to back the foundation and expand its work. His five genuine old masters and some minor works were divided between his two daughters, along with the remaining 25% of his substantial estate.

Called the Vergruen Reference Collection, the foundation now does two, or occasionally, three, traveling shows per year, and serves as a popular educational resource everywhere it's shown. Familiarly referred to in the art trade as the VRC, it draws the attention of scholars from all over the world. Novice collectors who see it often wish their own fakes were as good. A favorite pastime is trying to guess how each faked picture falls short of the original, which can be difficult, since only the best are included. Opinions can vary widely. Piet Vergruen would have been gratified.

CHAPTER 1

I've always had a weakness for fakes. It's not that I buy them, even by mistake. It's that in the sixteen years since I left art school, and even before that period, I've painted a fair number of them myself, just to learn the techniques of the masters. Of course, I always sign them *Paul Zacher* on the back. I don't know any better approach—when you paint a picture yourself, even one previously painted by another artist, you get inside it in ways that the viewer never can. When I look at the work of a forger, I love to observe what things he misunderstood about the painting that made his version come up short.

Naturally, it was with considerable excitement that I arrived at the Bellas Artes, one of our two prominent art schools here in San Miguel de Allende, México, to see sixty examples from the Vergruen Reference Collection in person. I was the first one to enter the exhibition gallery when it opened—not that there was much of a line.

The show was as good as I had hoped, and I was about two-thirds of the way through it, pausing here and there for long periods to examine pictures I was well acquainted with, when I stopped abruptly before one that I knew much more intimately than any of the others.

This picture was not a fake. It was the last thing

in the world I expected, and I stood in front of it for some time in astonishment.

Since I felt duped by having a great masterpiece of seventeenth century French painting substituted for a copy, I found myself in south central Texas the following afternoon trying to find out why. I don't like being cheated—don't try to palm off genuine on me when I'm expecting bogus.

The nameplate on the door in front of me said, *The Vergruen Reference Collection*, and below it, Dr. Bernhard Glass, Director. It was one of eight identical oak-veneered doors on the corridor. They were stained a reddish mahogany color, the nameplate itself dark olive plastic, the letters laser-cut into the white layer beneath. Only Dr. Glass's nameplate had serifs; it must have been a perk. I knocked twice and walked in. I had dressed for this visit in a fresh pair of chinos and a collar shirt under a light tan corduroy sport coat. This was as much credibility as I could muster on short notice. It was an outfit I've also worn to funerals, or to parties where I didn't know many people. San Miguel is not a formal town. I didn't know how formal this Dr. Glass was, but after all, he dealt in fakes, how stiff could he be?

The reception area was well furnished, but not luxurious, befitting a nonprofit institution dedicated to serious scholarship in the art of making fraudulent pictures. The woman who looked up from her desk gave me an encouraging nod of her head. She was not yet forty but I could see by her makeup and the way she dressed that she was trying to keep it at arm's length. I could sympathize—I was less than three years away from it myself. She had a serious manner, with thin lips and a long neck.

Looking spare and efficient, she was perfect for the sober task at hand; the protection and enlightenment of a gullible public. She must have guessed already that I was one of them.

"Mr. Zacher?"

"Yes, I'm here to see Dr. Glass."

"Of course. You're fortunate that he could meet with you this morning. You can go right in." She gestured to a door opposite the end of her desk.

With considerable surprise, ten seconds later I found facing me across the desk in the inside office a man I used to know as Professor Aaron H. Levi. During the final two years of my tenure at the art school of Miami University in Ohio, he was Professor A. Herschel Levi, since after his promotion to department chairman, and possibly in honor of that event, he had decided to reconfigure his name. After that the students all started calling him A, a letter that during his teaching days he had rarely given as a grade, but one he might have readily tolerated if he understood it as his rank on the faculty, or in life. I hadn't seen him in more than fifteen years, and I'd thought about him equally as often. He was a man who, once you got him out of your life, quickly receded into shadow like the nightmares of childhood. Now he was back in a way I found oddly uncomfortable. It was more than just a surprise.

To say he was full of himself understates the density of his self-esteem. His body, though substantial, simply could not accommodate his ego, which, as it escaped, expanded like an aura around him, often filling the room, and at times, as I recalled, an entire lecture hall.

Glass's head had always been shaped like a

pumpkin, with chipmunk cheeks, but now his chin was broader and his neck thicker, so that the whole construction seemed to sit on a more adequate base. He still wore the same florid style of bow tie, one he always let you know without saying so, perhaps just by tugging on it and drawing one end out farther, that he tied himself. You could never do that with the clip-on kind. This one was yellow with tiny fleur de lis in the weave. Although my manual skills are first class in many ways, I wouldn't have been able to tie a bow tie if I'd had four hands.

Showing no recognition, which was fine with me, he rose as I approached his desk and offered me a limp hand. As I took it, a painting on the wall behind him caught my eye. A rural scene with two stone cottages roofed in red tile, bare plowed fields in front, and a bank of trees off center behind. All this was arranged under a ragged sky. I knew it instantly as a Camille Pissarro from the period in the 1880s when he was becoming more Impressionistic in style. Glass's eyes followed mine.

"A fake, of course," he said, genially, "but quite a good one, if you know Pissarro's work." It was clear he didn't expect me to. "I'm Dr. Bernhard Glass. Fakes are what we do here." I wondered if he really meant it the way it came out.

Bernhard Glass was a name not less Jewish than his previous one, only more elegant, and I was always a bit suspicious of people with a Ph.D. who called themselves doctor. I suspected he was not using the new name to hide his Jewish background, but more to elevate it from his base beginnings. Had he briefly considered using Rothschild before he settled for Glass? It was clear that he didn't recognize me, and because I didn't want to be thrust backward into the role of art student, I didn't plan to bring up our prior connection. As before when I knew him, his bearing appeared to be opaque, aside from his self-absorption, and his new name did not make it more transparent. He wore his connoisseurship in a way that not only defined his professional life, but also veiled any other aspect of his character, except his ego. Dr. Blowhard Glass would have been a better name choice, but I felt it was too early in our conversation to suggest it. Even when I was an undergraduate, I'd felt that if he'd been able to turn all his insights into coin at once, the total pile would still have been small change.

"P. Zacher," I said, trying to obscure my own name in case he might remember it. Not likely, since he hadn't known me by name when I was in school. No news of my modest success in San Miguel would have reached him—even aided by a tail wind, it rarely reached the city limits. He gestured to the chair opposite his desk.

"My secretary said you had information that might be of interest to me," he said doubtfully, as if he already possessed all the information that was ever going to be of interest to him, and had given up searching for more. This hadn't changed over the years.

"I'll get right to the point," I said, "since I'm sure you're busy. I recently saw the Vergruen Reference Collection exhibition in San Miguel de Allende, México. The Georges de la Tour picture titled *St. Jerome* that you have on view there is definitely not a fake." I modestly folded my hands on my lap and waited for him to be devastated. No reaction was visible. He didn't even chuckle.

"And why would you think that could possibly be the case?" He took his time with this sentence, paying careful attention to each word as it dripped with irony.

"Dr. Glass, I'm a painter myself, and during my early years I painted the works of a number of old masters to study their technique. The *St. Jerome* is a picture I copied during that time, so I understand it quite well. When you study something in sufficient detail to reproduce it, you don't forget it, even the brushstrokes. La Tour was a master of the glow from a small, focused light source. This is well known, but what you won't read in the literature is that he was also clumsy with eyes and hands. Naturally you'd have to be a highly skilled painter to even attempt a copy, but if you were good enough to try it, the tendency would be to unconsciously correct his errors. I had to fight this inclination myself as I worked. The picture you're exhibiting in México doesn't correct them in any way."

"Then it seems to me that this would only suggest the forger was a more skillful copyist than you are. Isn't that equally possible?"

"Theoretically possible, but I don't believe that's the case here."

"I think you flatter yourself, young man." At thirty-seven, I actually enjoyed being called young man, even though I knew that in his vocabulary the word really meant *idiot.* This sounded so much like the old Professor Levi that I almost burst out laughing. He had said this many times to any student who had the nerve to think he'd painted a good picture.

"I make a good living as a painter and I don't need to flatter myself," I said. "It would only get in my way." This was partly true; the latter part.

"Then I think we will agree to disagree, but tell

me this." Here Glass leaned forward, as if about to skewer me. "The Vergruen Reference Collection is an important resource for scholars all over the world. How would it happen that no one else has come up with this *opinion*?" He stressed the last word as if it were contemptible, a kind of statement bordering on the obscene, or one you'd quickly want to scrape off the bottom of your shoe when no one was looking. Clearly he had no opinions himself; he dealt only in certainty.

"Maybe it hasn't been shown before in a VRC exhibit, so the word isn't out yet. Are you a painter, Dr. Glass?" I knew he wasn't. He may have taken one or two studio courses in getting his doctorate, but changing his name was the first creative spark I'd ever observed in him.

"My field is art history. If I may say so, it's a more comprehensive approach to the subject." He folded his arms defensively.

"Then you'll excuse me for saying that while you may have a broader view, you don't have a painter's eye, which is quite different from a historian's."

"I've observed people with what you call the painter's eye throughout my career, and I've seen it produce a great deal of horrendous work as well as some good efforts, most of which still fell somewhat short of the mark. I prefer the historian's eye as being more consistent. I know *mine* is. Scholars all over the world depend on it for good reason."

"I have just one more question then." I leaned forward at the edge of his desk, but without touching it. "Many of the pictures in the San Miguel show list the name of the donor. Some don't. The la Tour is one of those that doesn't reveal this. Can I ask why?"

"A simple reason." Grinning here, his voice took on a more patronizing tone, as if this were an aspect of curating the collection that anyone of even marginal intelligence would have known without asking. "Some of the connoisseurs who donate pictures to us are embarrassed by their error in judgment. They simply wish to forget it ever happened; therefore no provenance is given to the public. In the case of the la Tour, the collector is rather well known, and he didn't wish to have this single mistake color people's opinion about the rest of his holdings. As always, we respect that wish, since his other paintings may come up for auction at some point. Is there anything else? If not, I think we are finished here." Glass picked up a small sheaf of papers and tapped their bottom edge sharply on the desk surface. If he'd had a small guillotine at the side of his desk, my neck would have been in it. I sensed he valued closure.

I was dismissed as if the bell had rung at the end of the class period. No surprise. Dr. Glass had always been impressed by his own authority. I paused at the door and turned to face him. When I stopped, he looked up with a shadow of irritation darkening his broad face, and his forehead developed a cluster of lines over his nose. "That Pissarro on the wall behind you is genuine as well," I said, "and I think you know that. If you don't, you ought to." I closed the door quietly on his blank stare.

I hadn't intended to go that far, but then I had no idea I'd run into him again. As I walked back down the hall, I tried to think of ways I could have been more diplomatic, but the conversation would probably have come out the same. As it went down, it felt like the face-off I'd wanted to have with him several times when I was in college, one that had never happened because I wanted to graduate more. I wasn't a hundred percent sure about the Pissarro without a closer examination, but it seemed like a good finishing line. While I don't usually represent myself as an expert, this time it seemed like the only way to get through to him on terms he understood.

In any case, I still had no doubt about the la Tour, even though I had no idea whatever what was going on.

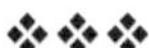

"Stonewalled," I said when I caught up with Cody and Maya back at the hotel. They'd just gotten back from lunch. Cody was my retired cop friend from Peoria. I'd known him since he moved to San Miguel de Allende seven years earlier. Maya was my longtime girlfriend. Together we formed the Zacher Agency, an occasionally successful detective shop that could still cause a lot of trouble for people even when we weren't. Often we only caused trouble for ourselves. This looked like it was shaping up into one of those times. I couldn't even have said what the point of this was, except that when people tell me something is a fake and it isn't, it makes me ask what the hell is really going on, since it's usually the other way around.

"What did you expect? That he would roll over and lick the Méxican dust off your shoes?" said Cody. He stood at the window of our fourth-floor room looking down at the sparse traffic in this middle-size Texas city. His 230-pound, six-foot-three bulk filled the frame. "You're throwing yourself against the high walls of academe here. For myself, I don't even know how you can be so certain."

"I can see it, is how. La Tour was light on anatomy. Jerome's knuckles don't work in that painting. The eyes are ever so slightly out of focus. I struggled to paint them that way myself, and it went against everything I know. You're going to have to trust me here. That picture is exactly what la Tour would have done, what he *did* do, in fact."

"But think about it; what would be the point of showing a genuine picture as a fake?" asked Maya, folding her arms like Cody had. She had just turned thirty, and today was wearing her sprayed-on jeans, with rhinestones forming a shield on both back pockets. Saying this, she pushed one leg out ahead of the other. I seemed to be evoking a lot of defensive reactions these days. Her look said it might be time to reel me in a bit before we got in over our heads again.

Last time that happened, less than a month ago, she'd been forced to kill someone who was waiting for me in our bed, and it didn't go well for me afterward. She still hadn't dealt with it completely. It made her more eager to challenge what I was thinking, not that she'd ever hesitated in the past.

"I don't know the reason. I only know that it was the real painting."

"Who's got it?" said Cody. "Or, rather, who had it?"

The labels at the VRC show also listed the location of the genuine painting, if only in some cases as "private collection."

"The tag at the exhibition said it's in the Minneapolis Academy of Art. I'd like to go up there and take a look at what they're showing as the la Tour. If it's missing, that'll settle it, or maybe they'll hire us to get it back when I prove they're showing a copy. Come on along, I don't want this to be just my show. We need a vacation anyway. That's why we came up here."

"Right." They said this doubtfully in unison, looking at each other but not at me. Sometimes they back me up, if I'm not too far off the wall, only because we all have to work together. Sometimes they still don't.

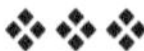

Minneapolis is not my favorite place. When I left southeastern Ohio in the nineties, one of the reasons I chose San Miguel to live is that it resembles, aside from the cars and the American tourists, a prosperous Méxican town of about 1700. We have no traffic lights, and the facades of buildings in the central district, by statute, are not permitted to be altered. It has recently become a UNESCO World Heritage site.

In Minneapolis, possibly by statute as well, no older buildings are permitted to survive, because their existence might slow down the ruthless pace of progress. Sites where they once stood are now parking lots or skyscrapers. No plaques are permitted to state what historic structure might have stood there. The impression is always that of moving on, looking forward, never glancing back. But to me this isn't progress; I think it's useful to know where you've been, because it helps in knowing where you're going. My view of the universe includes a sense of continuity; some people call it cause and effect.

You can't mention this part of the States without bringing up the climate. Maya and I had been in Minneapolis for a funeral two years before and I knew that, for five months every year, your exhaled breath freezes solid as it emerges from your nose and crashes to the icy pavement with a delicate tinkling sound, shattering on impact. Touch anything metal with your bare hands, and you are condemned to cling to it like a lover who deserted you for no good reason. On the weather maps during these periods, a nasty finger of Arctic air holds the place prostrate and unmoving. All squirming stops. Now we were back, in February, and it was my idea. I had even referred to this visit as a vacation. I didn't feel guilty, exactly. Perhaps stupid was a better word, but I was on a mission.

I won't even get into how it affected Maya. She grew up in México City, where zero was a figure she occasionally encountered in clusters of two or three on a check, but had to look up in the dictionary for any other application.

With the aid of a street map, we found the art academy fairly quickly and pulled into a parking space behind a Cadillac SUV. On the rear, a bumper sticker stated without embarrassment, "Minnesota—We Know What's Best for You."

"Sounds like an enlightened state," said Cody, nodding his head. "A lot of places never get to that point."

Certainly none in México ever had; the nanny culture is unknown there. Maya didn't understand it at all. Her lips were moving as she silently reread it. "I suppose," I said, "that Illinois isn't like that, too?"

"In Illinois it would have said, 'We know what's

best for you, and here's what it's going to cost you.'"

The Minneapolis Academy of Art looked like a mostly Stanford White building of the early twentieth century, puffed up with granite columns and chockfull of Beaux Arts optimism and high culture. I guessed that it had been cheerfully bought and paid for by recently emerged magnates in railroads, wheat, and banking. Grafted to one side and the rear are two additions, one from the early seventies, fortress-like in attitude as it confronts the threat of mushrooming civil disorder on the surrounding streets. The other is a more recent effort by Michael Graves, with the post-modern echoes he clings to as architectural styles continue to evolve. This is not a bad style—I think of it as ambiguously archaic, something I'm comfortable with because it suits my own mindset.

Inside, we quickly found the seventeenth century section, graced by a single example of Rembrandt's work—a portrait titled *Lucrecia*. The subject grips a bloody knife in her hand, having just inserted it into her breast. How she removed it afterward was not clear, but it now hangs listlessly at her side. A look of terminal dismay darkens her face. Technically superb, emotionally poignant, it was a melancholy masterpiece that had probably hung in the donor's study for a while until he couldn't stand it anymore, then shipped it off to the Minneapolis Academy of Art for the tax deduction. Across the room from it was an approximate version of Georges de la Tour's *St. Jerome*. It gained no credibility from facing a Rembrandt twenty-five feet away.

I had taken special care examining the San Miguel version of this picture from the Vergruen Reference Collection show. My visual memory is exact, coming from many long exercises in the studio of continuing to paint the human figure or portrait when the subject was on rest break, or gone for lunch. Although when I copied this picture I had substituted a pool cue for Jerome's gnarled staff, since the painting was commissioned for a client's billiard room, I had replicated the hands as they were in the original. The pool cue, of course, was narrower than the staff, so Jerome's grip was looser in my version.

I looked first at those hands. As in the one in San Miguel, the fingers were grubby and blunt, but in this version the segments of the fingers came off each other properly and both eyes looked back over my shoulder in the same direction, possibly studying the Rembrandt.

"Looks OK to me," said Cody. "I don't see a problem."

"That's exactly what's wrong with it;" I replied, "you *nailed* the problem. This is the one that should have been in the show. Look at his hands, look at the eyes. It's a subtle thing, but these are all correct. Unconsciously, the person who forged this painting couldn't make himself replicate la Tour's errors. Maybe he didn't even know they were there—sometimes your eye will automatically correct things, or maybe it wasn't in his nature to paint them badly."

"The saint's hands are still dirty," said Maya, with a shrug. Her position was that all art should be beautiful, so you started with a beautiful subject to get you halfway there right out of the gate. All you had to do then was not screw it up.

"Even so." I walked over to the guard in the doorway who was trying not to appear to be listening to our conversation. We should have had it in Spanish. "Where are the offices, please?"

"Back in the lobby you'll find a stairway to the left of the desk." As we moved off, he drifted over towards the la Tour with a frown.

I led the others back to the lobby and we climbed the stairs. In the director's office, we were told by the receptionist that he was in Europe on a buying trip with one of the museum's biggest patrons, the heir to one of the department store chains.

"Does he have an executive assistant?" I said.

"That would be Clarissa Phelps. I'll see if she can talk to you." She picked up her phone.

A moment later a tall dark-haired woman in a mauve silk blouse and black wool slacks emerged from a side office. I placed her age at about forty-five. We introduced ourselves and she shook hands with each of us. "Please come into my office," she said. Her fingers were long and elegant, and on the middle one of her left hand was an antique cameo ring set in yellow gold. Although the setting was simple and possibly recent, the stone might have been Roman. If not, then it was a Renaissance copy. Her attitude was friendly and helpful.

Inside her office, the furnishings were minimal modern. We all sat on a leather sofa and she faced us leaning against her desk. The dark green walls were covered with old architectural engravings from the museum's paper art collection.

"So," she said. "How can I help you?" She sounded like she really believed she could.

"I have reason to believe that one of your pictures is a fake," I said, expecting outrage, although I didn't go as far as shielding my face.

"It wouldn't be the first time," she said, smiling. "Which one are you thinking of?"

"The Georges de la Tour *St. Jerome*."

Her smile faded, and she hesitated before she went on. "That's a *very* valuable painting, and our only example of his work. Not that many survive. What would make you think that?"

"For starters," I said, "I recently saw the real one in México."

"Are you an expert?" she said, nodding.

"In a way. I'm a painter." She relaxed a bit, smiling again as if the threat had faded. What would a painter know? No intelligent person would ever voluntarily be one, and their ranks were swelled by pitiful hacks and glib charlatans. With all the painters I had known, I mostly agreed with this view myself.

"That would certainly qualify you to be an expert on your own work, but would it apply as well to seventeenth century French painting?" Cody and Maya were looking increasingly uncomfortable, as if their chosen spokesperson was a known crackpot once again being caught in the process of proving it.

"It would in this case, Ms. Phelps. I've copied that painting, so I know it intimately. If you've done that, you don't forget the detail."

"So you've seen the original before? Worked from it? It's been in our collection for more than thirty years, and I don't recall that we ever issued a permit for someone to copy it here, and I would be the one signing off on that. Of course, I haven't been here that long, myself."

"I worked with an archival reproduction from Skirra based on a photograph. The colors and details were all correct, and it was actual size."

She thought for a moment, looking out the single window onto Third Avenue South.

"I certainly want to thank you for coming forward with this information, but what exactly is your interest in this, Mr. Zacher, if I may ask?"

"At this point I'm not sure. Possibly I could help you get the original back. I sometimes get involved in detective matters. Quite discreetly, of course. No one else would have to be aware of this problem."

A tolerant smile crossed her lips. Now she knew my game.

"And you say you saw the original in México. Was it in a private collection? Something a person would have for his own enjoyment?"

"On the contrary, it was exhibited publicly, and labeled as a fake. I saw it in the Vergruen Reference Collection two days ago."

Again her smile disappeared, her lips tightening into a narrow line.

"The VRC was here last summer." Clarissa Phelps said this in monotone, as if mumbling to herself, not looking at us.

Alarms went off in my brain. She was shaking her head now. "It was a huge success. We sold a lot of tickets for it. People always love fakes. I think it's the thought of all the experts and wealthy collectors they once fooled." She sat down behind her desk for the first time, rubbing her wrist thoughtfully, then reached up to smooth out the lines that had appeared in the center of her forehead. "I did my thesis on Fragonard and his teachers, so I know something about French painting, even though la Tour is earlier than the period I was writing about. I know you're sincere about this, but I really can't believe it. If you want to know the truth, I just don't want to believe it."

"Was this la Tour among the counterfeit paintings on exhibit by the Vergruen when it was here?" asked Cody, speaking up for the first time. His body language suggested it was not more than a casual question of no great importance.

"I knew one of you was going to ask that. No, it wasn't, but remember, the Vergruen holdings include more than a thousand pieces now. No more than a fraction of them are on the road at any time. It's become an archive as much as a traveling museum. It's also in the process of becoming a cultural institution. Some would say it already is. The current director has made a very strong mark in the field of forgeries."

I held my face in a carefully controlled, neutral mask.

"But wouldn't it have been a nice touch to include it for their show, since you own the original?" asked Maya. "You could have shown them side by side. It would have been a striking contrast, wouldn't it, since the VRC's mission is educating people about fakes? I can't think of a way to make the point better." It was at times like this that Maya could put her finger right on an important nuance of the issues. She was right, and I had missed this one.

Clarissa Phelps shrugged uneasily. "That's true, but it's likely that they don't know our collection that well. It was possibly only an oversight on their part."

"But you have your catalogue online, don't you?" I asked. "I checked this before I came up here, and I think it states that the database includes your entire collection.

It would have been easy for them to see if their holdings had any overlap, and assemble their show to take advantage of it. I assume they chose the contents of their show."

"They did, and I don't have a good answer for that." On her desk pad she flipped a tiny fleck of dust into oblivion. "You raise an excellent point, but I think you'd have to contact them directly and ask them why they didn't." A good suggestion, but I knew Glass would never allow me in his office again after my parting remark, or even take my calls.

"Is this something you could look into?" I asked. "I've already had a conversation with the VRC director about the la Tour. I may have been insufficiently diplomatic when we talked, and we're not speaking anymore."

"I'm afraid I don't have the authority to do that. It would have to come from our director, but I'll bring it up with him when he gets back."

"When will that be?" asked Maya.

"He'll be back in the office on the thirteenth. He's attending three auctions in Paris."

That was in eight days. We thanked her, I gave her my landline number in San Miguel, and we left.

"Not much outrage there," said Cody, when we got back on the street, rubbing his finger across his lips before he put his glove back on. "Your news certainly didn't cause her to start circling the wagons, I'll give her credit for that."

Maya pulled her collar up around her neck and shivered as the wind hit us.

"Unlike Bernhard Glass," I said, "I think she's being straight on this and she'll really bring it up with the director. I saw no resistance on her part either, just nervous interest."

"How interested is the director going to be in exposing it if it's a fake?" asked Cody. "It seems like they've got a reputation to protect. This whole building expresses their authority and connoisseurship, not their gullibility. Everything their collection stands for is the opposite of the VRC."

The third morning after we returned to San Miguel, Maya went to the market, the new Mega that had replaced the old Gigante as our regular food store. It was better organized, but she couldn't find certain things now. The caviar was no longer next to the tires, not that we bought much of it except at the end of difficult cases, and we walked too much to need new tires very often. When she returned, she slapped a copy of *Atención*, our bilingual newspaper, down on the counter as she unpacked the groceries.

"Paul, look at this!" she said, placing her finger on the headline. BREAK-IN AT THE BELLAS ARTES, it read. It went on to relate how burglars had entered the Vergruen Reference Collection show after hours and removed a forgery of the famous Georges de la Tour painting titled *St. Jerome.* The police were perplexed because the show had clearly been titled *Great Fakes and Forgeries*. The value of the stolen picture was given as 5,000 pesos—about $400. I had spent some time on the Internet and I knew that based on la Tour's most recent auction results, which were as sparse as his surviving paintings, the picture was probably worth between four and seven million dollars. I ran the article through my scanner and emailed it to Clarissa Phelps without comment.

"This does something for your tattered credibility," said Maya.

"Oh ye of little faith," I said. "I see two possibilities here. One, someone else recognized it like I did, and took advantage of the minimal security to cart it off; or two, Bernhard Glass decided I was too much of a pain and had it removed himself before I made more trouble, so that no one could back me up. I know which one I favor, because now we'll never be able to prove it's real. Now it can disappear without much fanfare."

"And the Minneapolis Academy of Art will never hire us to get it back. We don't have a client."

"Nothing new about that. We'll work *pro bono*."

I thought I heard her mutter the words, *Boy Scout case*, her term for expending our efforts on a situation where no one paid us, and we received no thanks. Internal rewards were not her thing; she would have preferred a sash with emeralds on it and a public tribute.

CHAPTER 2

While Maya put away the groceries, I went down to the Bellas Artes to examine the crime scene. Going in I found that the edge of the street door on Hernandez Macias had been fractured and already repaired by replacing the plank at the edge and remounting a new lock. Inside, the door to the large exhibition hall next to the chapel (the Bellas Artes had for centuries been a convent until the dispersal of the nuns in the 1920s) had been subjected to the same treatment. The show was now closed and a guard stood at the door.

After our last case, where we had saved the State of Guanajuato from a major environmental disaster, Licenciado Diego Delgado of the San Miguel Judicial Police had given each of us an impressive certificate on police letterhead certifying that we were licensed private investigators, although no legal process existed to certify us. It was more like something we would have gotten from the chamber of commerce, like the key to the city. It had only taken seven or eight cases for Delgado to come to the conclusion that a credential of some kind could be helpful, since we had mostly tried to avoid stepping on his toes. He had the innate delicacy to avoid mentioning the fact that the governor of the state of Guanajuato and his successor had both been killed in that last affair. We all thought of it as our sloppiest effort, since only luck had saved us from being killed ourselves. Cody especially thought that, if it was only luck that saved us, we'd better go back and spend some time with the manuals before we took on another case.

We'd possibly received these certificates because all the other bad guys in the plot had also died, saving Delgado's office a lot of time in the courts, as well as volumes of paperwork. It gave me a certain official credibility that none of us in the Zacher Agency had ever had, except Cody, when he was still a cop in Peoria. I showed this document to the guard, who studied it in detail before handing it back. I knew he'd never seen anything to compare it to.

"I'd like to ask you a few questions," I said. He nodded. "Was anyone on duty when the break-in occurred?"

"No. Their budget doesn't provide for after-hours security. We just lock the doors at the end of the day." He shrugged. "Besides, who would want to steal these pictures? It's not like they're the real thing, you know? I don't usually do this myself; I was just hired by the Vergruen people for the length of the show. Normally I deliver bottled water."

"Were any of the other paintings disturbed?"

"No, only that one."

"The frame was taken too, or was it cut out?"

"The frame is gone too. I heard someone say it was probably more valuable than the painting."

"Has anyone from the Vergruen Reference Collection talked to you about it?"

"Not to me personally, but possibly to the

director. You'd have to ask her."

"When will the show reopen?"

"In a day or two." In México this could mean three or four days, or a week. Specific numbers become estimates, days become weeks.

I thanked him and went to the administration suite. Bellas Artes Directora María Torres received me in her office and asked me to sit down while she examined my new credential. It wouldn't be of much use in talking to private citizens, but with any official in México it was valuable. I expressed my shock and outrage at the burglary and she nodded sadly as she handed it back to me. "It is the first time we have had a problem since I came here," she said. "The only good thing is that the stolen picture was of no serious monetary value, but of course, we are embarrassed nonetheless. We have this show in trust."

I was not about to suggest what the value of the missing picture really was.

"I only have one question. I assume you notified the director of the Vergruen immediately the next morning. Have any of them followed up with you?" I was trying to assess how Glass was playing this.

"Nothing since my first conversation with Dr. Glass, but it's only been three and a half days." No time at all in México.

"Is the collection insured?"

"That would be two questions," she said with a smile. "But the insurance was only for fire, not theft. I don't think they imagined that anyone would break in to steal a single forgery. What would be the point?"

"I have no idea; thank you very much, *señora.*"

Outside in my new Town and Country van (my old artmobile had been blown into the hereafter in an attempt on my life on our last case, taking the bomber with it), I dialed Licenciado Delgado. We went through the usual courtesies.

"Anything new on the burglary at the Bellas Artes?" I said.

"Nothing. But you are now imagining that this is at the top of my priorities, what with the recent murder? I may have to reconsider that certificate I gave you. Maybe it is already expired, who knows? Do you see a date stamped on it anywhere?"

Of course Delgado had put no expiration date on it. While I was regarding it as perpetual, he must have been thinking it was conditional, depending on whether I served him the Don Eduardo Añejo tequila when he came over, or the Cuervo, which we used for the maid's and the gardener's birthdays. Whether I kept him in the loop on what I was working on, or not.

"Murder?" I said, correctly identifying the only meaningful word in his statement.

"Yes. You are surprised you have not already been called in on it?"

"Moderately. After all, I often am before you are."

"Those would mostly be on the killings you do yourself, I believe. Occasionally other people call us first."

"Not everyone's got my number," I said, glad of that.

"No, but I do. As for your question, a man named Carlos Ortíz was found at the side of the Celaya road last night, near the dam on the way to Comonfort. He had been dead for a while, and we don't have the autopsy results yet."

"Any criminal record?"

"A minor *ladron*, arrested four times for breaking and entering, with two convictions. *Papas pequeñas*, (small potatoes), as you would say in Gringolandia."

"Was he shot?"

"Twice in the back of the head. It appears to be an execution."

"What else do you have?"

"Nothing. No gun, no marks at the scene to guide us. The body was mostly hidden by bushes, and discovered by school children waiting for a bus. We found no blood present, so we are thinking the actual murder was committed elsewhere."

"How was he dressed?"

"All in black."

"I am thinking now of the break-in at the Bellas Artes. Any reason to connect Ortíz with that?"

"He had no forged painting with him. What else would there be? In the past he always took cash and jewelry. I don't think he was connected to the theft at the Bellas Artes."

"Did he usually work alone?"

"As far as we know. On his previous arrests no one else was with him that we could find."

"You recovered the bullets?"

"Yes. They are being analyzed."

"How about his wallet?"

"Absent. He was identified by his fingerprints. Many are on record to choose from."

"In the spirit of our long history of cooperation, I should tell you something more," I said. I could almost hear his eyebrows go up on the other end. "The painting that was stolen from the Bellas Artes show was not a fake."

Silence. Had the mutilated fan above his head been moving, I would've also heard its breathy whisper.

"While I'm sure that many of your pictures are of museum quality, Señor Zacher, I wonder if that qualifies you as an expert on the work of others? Particularly those long dead, and in this case, French? Do you see? I know this."

Essentially the same reaction I'd had from Clarissa Phelps and Bernhard Glass. The three formed an unlikely combination. I repeated the story of copying the picture, the same one that had convinced no one in the past. Credibility is important here. Mine comes and goes, and it's usually at low ebb when I need it.

"Well, we will see. If we recover the picture, I will order it examined by another expert of the art. In the meantime let me know if you have any other ideas."

"I'll let you know when I solve it. How about that?" I said, starting my engine as I signed off. I didn't want to push Delgado, but I thought he was riding a little too high in the saddle for what little he knew. It was clear to me that Ortíz must have been the burglar. Breaking and entering could be a high-risk occupation; we had done it ourselves often enough, but it was risky mainly when the perp was interrupted by the homeowner or the police. This looked more like a cover-up. Any homeowner who caught a burglar and shot him would probably fire only one round, and then call the police rather than move the body out to the countryside and dump it in the bushes.

This left me in an interesting position. Aside from Glass, who had acknowledged nothing, no one knew about the la Tour being genuine except the three of us in the agency, and Clarissa Phelps, saving the equivocal reaction of Delgado. Of course, I wasn't sure how much credence Clarissa would give the idea until she could get into it further when the director returned. Possibly Maya and Cody didn't give it much either. Ortíz's murder might change that. Other people may appreciate fakes as I do, but they don't kill for them.

Back at home I stared for a while at the two Diego Riveras I'd copied when I first came to San Miguel. They were right on. Probably not even Frida Kahlo could have distinguished them from the real ones in her husband's studio without looking at the back, where I had signed them with my own name. I was not going to budge on the la Tour.

That afternoon I was cleaning some brushes when the phone rang. It was Clarissa Phelps, sooner than I'd expected.

"I had an odd meeting this morning and I wanted to let you know about it," she said. "A man named Charles Benoist asked to see the director, and when I talked to him instead, he told me that the touches of viridian green in the la Tour were not made from ground malachite, as they would have been in la Tour's time, but instead contained phthalo green, a modern pigment not developed until the 1860s. Things like this happen from time to time, when experts come through."

I sensed that I hadn't been included in this group. I also hadn't noticed this problem myself when I examined the picture. Style and technique, rather than paint chemistry, are my areas of expertise.

"Was he certain?" Malachite had gotten so expensive that it was almost never used in pigments anymore. I'd never seen it offered at Lagundi or Señor Pato, where I got my supplies.

"As much as he could be without UV tests. Benoist is a professor of art at The Sorbonne in Paris and his specialty is restoration. As you can imagine, I was stunned, thinking right away about your visit, and then his comment coming so soon after. I've ordered the picture removed and taken to our lab. I don't think the director will object when he gets back. I was basing this on the professor's comments, not yours. No offense."

Of course not—the man must have a Ph.D.

"None taken," I said. "Then let me emphasize something else. As you probably saw from the clipping I faxed to you, the la Tour I identified as genuine in the Vergruen Collection has been stolen from the show here. That was your picture. That was the second time it's been stolen recently. It's gotten very popular. I think it was stolen this time by the same person to get it out of view because I'd noticed it."

Silence. Then she took a deep breath.

"I wasn't really sure how to interpret that." She paused as if trying to make up her mind about something, and I could hear the tapping of a pen or pencil on her desktop. "What are your rates for detective work, Mr. Zacher? I'll see if I can reach the director now. Can I put you on hold?"

When I got off the phone I found Maya in the garden starting a Robert Crais mystery. Our detective adventures had sent her off in a new direction in her reading.

"We're back in business," I said. "The Minneapolis Academy of Art and the Zacher Agency have come to terms. As the head of the agency I need you to draw up a contract and fax it to Clarissa Phelps."

"Great," she said brightly. "And it looks like no one dies in this one, right? It's only about art."

As if to say, who cares about art? No one would ever kill for it.

"Not exactly. There's one already dead if my theory is correct. A convicted burglar named Carlos Ortíz was found murdered last night on the Celaya road."

"Hit and run?"

"It was definitely a hit and someone probably ran, but not the in way you mean. He had two bullets in his head."

"Oh." There was no enthusiasm in her tone. "And this connects to the theft at the Bellas Artes how?"

"It's a cover-up. Why else kill a burglar if you didn't catch him in the act? He had to have stolen the la Tour."

"But he didn't have it with him?"

"Of course not. He gave it to whoever hired him. He must have thought his part was over."

"I've made that mistake too. Now *you're* all over this one, aren't you?"

"Every bit of it. You know how phony art gets me going."

"So what's next?"

"No idea. We just do the contract and collect the down payment."

"So it's like all the other cases."

"Pretty much, but this time we serve the cause of Art, a higher calling."

The capitalization was all mine.

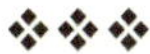

"From what I recall of the size, it would just about fit in most car trunks," said Cody, as the three of us sat down for *comida* late that afternoon at Harry's New Orleans Bar. "It could be anywhere now. Even over the border at this point." He raised three fingers to the waiter.

"Right," I said. "The border guards wouldn't know it from a Thomas Kinkaid, where there's a light in every window. And the U.S. has no duty on paintings. Customs would pass it through with no questions."

"But what was the point of putting it in the show here?" asked Maya, after thinking for a moment.

"Being part of that show would certify it as a fake, I guess, since it's listed in the show catalog as one." The waiter came back and distributed three margaritas to stimulate creative thinking. "Then you can carry it around in public anywhere and no one notices, just like any other fake once it entered the Vergruen Reference Collection. I think that's a big plus. It also suggests that Glass has someone in the background capable of reproducing a picture like that. No easy task, as I know from having done it myself."

"Now isn't that an interesting thought," said Cody, leaning forward with his massive elbows on the table. "What if this is about more than just that single la Tour? What if Glass has got a system? After all, it worked pretty well until you tripped them up."

"You mean there could be other genuine paintings in the show?" I asked.

"That's what I'm thinking. Didn't Clarissa Phelps

say that the Vergruen Reference Collection has about a thousand paintings, and only a small portion travel at any time? I think we need some research here. What if we could cross-reference the recent shows of the VRC with the collections of the museums they were shown at? If we find any overlap, then see if some of the forgeries on view here in San Miguel match originals from any of those places. Paul, you could examine those pictures in detail and see what we've got. It would be like expert testimony."

Although I was the one pushing to get involved with the VRC, I was not deeply moved by this idea. "I don't know. I only knew that la Tour because I'd painted a copy of it. The same wouldn't apply to anything else. I wouldn't know the detail well enough on any other picture. Wait, but if we had such a list of the ones that appear in both places, we could get the archival reproductions from Skirra, like the one I used for my la Tour copy and start from there. But if they were the real thing I still couldn't tell from them whether anything was wrong, only that everything was right. It wouldn't be conclusive."

"But short of going around to half a dozen museums all over the world, it might be a good start."

"I'm on it," said Maya. As a historian, research was her game.

CHAPTER 3
NATTY BOLLANDER

Natty (don't call me Nate) Bollander was an Englishman who had been employed for fifteen years as a piecework art restorer for the Uffizi and Palazzo Pitti museums in Florence. Occasionally his workload was swelled by projects from the Paris auction houses. He lived next to his studio in a sixteenth century building almost overlooking the Arno. If he stood and looked diagonally down the side street he faced, he could see a sliver of it. His quarters on the third floor of the former warehouse, once belonging to the Medici family, were high enough above the water to have escaped any damage from the great flood of 1966. It wouldn't have mattered to Natty since he had been a small child in Bristol at the time.

From adolescence Natty had longed to be a painter, and like many fired with that ambition, his originality did not match his drive. As his technical skills grew at an impressive rate, his ability to generate the ideas to express with his brush advanced not at all. He was not drawn to Abstract Expressionism with its abandonment of drawing and representation. Instead, as he progressed, he compensated for his lack of ideas by mastering every technique he could observe in English museums, from the late Middle

Ages to late Victorian Pre-Raphaelites and post-Impressionists, thinking that with an unimpeachable level of skill, he couldn't possibly be a bad painter. By the late eighties he could have worked as a restorer at any museum in the world, but no commercial gallery had ever knowingly exhibited a painting of his, although many hung in art museums, none with his signature.

Florence was an obvious choice for a job in restoration. Natty was a master of everything except his own work, which contained elements of all the great styles of the past and yet had no coherent focus of its own. He was nothing more than a mechanic, albeit a great one, and some people who did not manage museums nonetheless had uses for an expert mechanic. A few had approached him early on.

Tall, with blond, collar-length hair, carrying some extra weight on his barrel chest that had not yet settled downward to his stomach, he wore a Van Dyke goatee and was partial to well-worn corduroy sport jackets on cool evenings. When he smoked a pipe, which was often when he wasn't working, he favored the Dunhill tobacco he bought in quantity on his semiannual return trips home. He had never gotten used to the Italian pipe blends, although he thought the English had a great deal to learn from the Italians about coffee. Even though his body had gotten bulky with maturity, his fingers were long and delicate, capable of great finesse with a brush. He also used them to play his girlfriend, Chiara, like a harp. She believed he was an artist. He never contradicted her.

Like many Italians in that Renaissance town, Chiara lived far from the historic center in a tiny expensive apartment where she didn't spend much time, preferring café life on long evenings at closer-in piazzas. This was how she had met Natty. The money that remained after she bought groceries and paid her rent went mostly for clothes and costume jewelry. She couldn't afford a car, but she always looked great. Thirty-one years old, with black eyes and hair worn layered and long, she always attracted admiring stares from the men seated around her in the cafes. She brushed them off easily; it came with the territory. Chiara spent as many nights at the former Medici warehouse as she did at her apartment, but Natty had never asked her to marry him or even to move in with him. If he had, she would have cancelled her lease and bought a small used Fiat with the savings. She believed it was the demanding character of his work that kept him from asking, and his tendency to paint long hours in silence when he had an important commission. Most of the time she hoped Natty would marry her, but it never seemed to come up. For seven years she had worked at the local office of a boring insurance company that was headquartered in Milan, processing claims. If she were married, perhaps she could quit.

If she thought it odd that Natty never worked on anything contemporary, mainly making copies of older paintings she had never seen, she said nothing, having confidence that one day he would break out and demonstrate his mastery on something of his own. How could he not? He was so talented.

Chiara loved the smell of his pipes, although they tended to blacken his teeth. Like many Italian women, she was prepared to accept certain eccentricities in her man. Besides, Natty always had more than enough money, and she had heard this was not typical of painters. She didn't know any others, but she could imagine it was true because the same problem also applied to nearly everyone she knew.

On a morning in late February she left the warehouse and walked to work, crossing the Ponte Vecchio, pausing now and then to look at the jewelry displays. The sky was misty and gray with a promise of rain.

Back in his studio, Natty returned to work on a copy of a late van Gogh for his American client. It was almost beneath his skill level; anyone could copy a van Gogh, and many had. He had seen a dozen fakes in various English museums; he even knew of one that had been auctioned to a Tokyo buyer for more than $70 million. What a dream job that had been! Although he suspected the painter who actually made the picture hadn't gotten much for it.

Other than a canvas of the correct age, scraped back down to the weave, all it took was a great deal of paint made from the older formulas, laid on in wide, splashy strokes. Of course they took a long time to dry, and required more curing time than other things he copied. It would be six months before it was ready to ship; it wouldn't do to have the paint skinned over but still spongy to the touch if it was supposed to be 130 years old. Like any forger who took his work seriously, Natty worked from the archival Skirra prints, and used the same brand of Dutch pigments van Gogh himself had used, still formulated in the same manner.

His only recent slip-up had been using phthalo green instead of malachite on the Georges de la Tour, but he couldn't locate any ground malachite on short notice, and after all, who would know? Because his emphasis was on masterful technique, he sometimes skimped on technical details. As he worked on the van Gogh, what he wanted to be doing was a portrait of Chiara, but he couldn't find the appropriate classical model to base it on. Maybe that Leonardo portrait of a woman with a dog could work, but Chiara didn't own a dog and didn't like them. Natty had no idea what to substitute in the space the dog occupied in the original. Certainly not a baby; he had a horror of children.

Just after noon he finished the van Gogh and added the signature, "Vincent" in that childishly naive way that van Gogh had always used. Something about the man had never grown up, and he had killed himself when still in his thirties without selling more than one or two pictures. Natty rolled up the Skirra print and slid it into his pigeonholed rack before cleaning his brushes. Dr. Bernhard Glass would be pleased, as he had always been for the past ten years.

As Natty was wiping off his hands, the phone rang.

"Dr. Glass here, Natty. How is it going?" Glass never called himself Bernhard.

"Very well, the van Gogh is finished, but I can't ship it to you until August."

"That's fine. Our show in San Francisco doesn't open until October, but I'm glad you're ready for another project because I've got a blockbuster for you."

"I hope I can get it from Skirra."

"Forget Skirra, they won't have this one."

"But they make a point of having all the great museum pictures in the western world. It's almost true."

"I know, but this time it's going to be a church

picture you're doing."

Natty stood silently for a while, thinking it might be an altar triptych. Some fabulous ones survived still in place in northern Europe. "Which one is it?" he asked finally.

"I'll tell you when you get on location. I want you to fly to México City next week and do the project there. It's not the kind of thing you want to be taking across the border. When you're finished with it, take a first class bus to Guadalajara. It's only about eight hours away. Get a hotel there. Bring Chiara with you this time. I'll cover it; we've been doing well lately. Call me when you're checked in."

Chiara would be happy, Natty thought after hanging up. She did have a few weeks of vacation coming and she'd never been to México. Surely the weather would be an improvement on the drizzly Italian winter.

CHAPTER 4

Although Maya had been busy, nothing more happened on my end for a week or so. I was working on a series of copies of eighteenth century Latin American devotional pictures based on a recent show catalogue from Philadelphia. The client, who owned a painstakingly correct restoration of a mid nineteenth century house in Guadalajara, liked the look of old saints staring mournfully up at the heavens. He didn't care, however, for the peeled, battered, and rippling old canvases they were painted on. He didn't want to see areas of the wall behind them when they were punctured. Nor did he appreciate paint flaking off and falling on his immaculate tile floors. Art is inevitably a casualty of age, and often of revolution. No shortage of that here. Copying paintings seemed to fit right in with this case, although for this group I found myself dulling down the pigments with raw sienna to get the look right. Brown gravy is not my normal palette.

I had met this client briefly when I delivered his first purchase two years before, and I knew he collected more recent work too, but he was not impressed when I showed him images of what I did, other than by the copies I'd done of other painters. I got the sense he liked things with a well-known name on them. Paul Who? It wasn't up to the mark.

In her research, Maya had turned up seven pictures, including the la Tour, held by museums that had recently hosted the Vergruen Reference Collection and that now also appeared in our local show. Cody and I were both surprised she'd found that many. Skirra had been able to supply prints of all of them by overnight air service and I was just unwrapping the parcel when the phone rang. It was Clarissa Phelps calling from the Minneapolis Academy of Art.

"It's no go, Paul, and somehow I'm not surprised," she said. Using my first name made it seem like we were now on the same side. "The director is back and he just isn't buying it anymore. I think he had a chance to go over it in his mind on the flight home. He shut me down right away and ordered the la Tour rehung. I got the feeling that he didn't want the publicity of finding a fraud in the collection. He even made reference to a media frenzy. Personally, I don't think the papers often care that much about art. Usually I have to work to get their attention."

"But what about the UV tests?"

"They did indicate phthalo green, but the director said they were only 80% accurate and it wasn't enough to go on. He said impurities often appeared in malachite that might give that result."

"Are you still thinking it's fake?"

"I'm inclined to. I even told him more detail about our conversation, although I already knew at that point he'd dismiss it, but to me, the UV test was confirmation."

"What now?"

"Nothing, I guess. I've got a job to keep here and

you're off the case. He had authorized the expenditure for your original retainer, but now nothing more. I'm emailing you a letter canceling our contract. Sorry. I'll let you know if anything more develops here, but I think the whole thing is just going to be paved over like a pothole here in spring."

Feeling like I should have been more consoling in my response to her, I went back to the Skirra package, but Clarissa Phelps knew what she had to do. No one wanted to know what I knew; I was just a person bursting with useless information—hardly an unusual condition. We would stay on the case, but for any expenses beyond the $500 retainer, we'd be working for free; also not a unique condition for an artist, but not that comfortable for an investigator. As with many of the donors to the Vergruen Reference Collection who wished to remain anonymous, the facts could be too embarrassing. I spent the rest of the day out in the loggia studying the prints in minute detail.

The next day, one of only four remaining for the show, we went back to the Bellas Artes and sought out the six pictures remaining of the seven that had come up on Maya's search. I hadn't tried to commit to memory all the detail on every one. Instead I focused on key items like hands and faces, and the quality of the light. In the two landscapes, it was also the character of the detail in the foliage, which was usually hard to replicate. Foliage demands a unique shorthand for every painter; and so each has his own signature technique, based on how much detail to render and how to render it. Part of it is also how the painter represents the larger, less-defined shadowy masses in the background. I had called earlier to see if I could bring the prints with me, but as usual, they didn't allow any parcels in the show, thinking, I suppose, that one might conceal an umbrella I could use to puncture the pictures.

I also had another theory I wanted to check out. It was that none of these six pictures would have a donor listed, because their history could be checked if they did. Maya and Cody stood behind me, waiting. We didn't speak until we got back outside on Hernandez Macias more than an hour later.

"All six are real," I said, "as far as I can tell. Nothing differs from the reproductions in the areas I studied. You'd think that out of that many, something would appear on at least one or two that wasn't quite right if they were fakes. Also, none of these six lists a donor, something that two-thirds of the others do. That doesn't prove anything in itself, but it suggests the way this is going."

"Then I can only think of one thing," said Cody. "We set a trap for them. We go public with the information that six genuine old masters are salted among the legitimate fakes, besides the stolen la Tour. It'll draw them out again, this time with a new burglar, or a crew of them, since six is a big number to remove."

"I suppose we'll have to shoot them, then," said Maya, without enthusiasm, not looking at either of us, "and then we'll narrowly avoid going to prison, again. And afterward, no one will pay us." As the head of the agency, she signed the checks.

"Possibly," I said, "but what I'd rather do is steal the pictures back from them in transit, since nobody believes us and we can't walk back into the show and lift them ourselves. But if we recover them once they're stolen, or at least taken down, we have a more compelling case to make to the museums that lost them when we offer their return. What do you think?"

"I like it," said Maya. "The publicity will make it impossible for the museums to dodge the issue. We'll be heroes."

"One thing to remember, though," said Cody. "The last burglar involved in this was murdered, if your theory is correct, and I think it probably is. If this works, they're going to throw everything they've got at us."

"Piffle," I said.

"The last time you said piffle, ten people died," said Maya. "You have a tendency to underestimate risk."

"Good point."

However it was not as if we could get a story about genuine paintings embedded in the VRC exhibit on the front page of *The New York Times*, even if there hadn't been all the Iraq and Afghanistan headlines. It was going to have to be our local *Atención* or nothing. We were all thinking the same thing.

"It's going to be a tough sell," said Cody, shaking his head.

"Maybe not. It isn't like important new stories are sprouting from the cobblestones here."

Cindy Foster had been the editor and publisher of our bilingual newspaper, *Atención*, since before I arrived in San Miguel. She'd interviewed me after two of our cases, so it looked like I was going to be the point man in getting her attention. She had also told me she'd always wanted to be a reporter during her career as an English teacher back in Tennessee. An inheritance made her retirement in San Miguel at forty possible, and provided the opportunity to buy the paper. Today was Tuesday; Friday was the day the weekly *Atención* came out. We might still make the deadline.

Cody dropped Maya back home and I walked over to the English Library and climbed the stairs in back to the Atención offices. As I bypassed the front counter, Cindy Foster looked up from her desk in the next room. Aside from a secretary and the girl covering the walk-in traffic, she was the only one present, but it wasn't a one-person operation, four other desks stood unoccupied nearby.

"Paul Zacher! How wonderful! You're coming to me with a story voluntarily now, right?"

"Hard to get anything past you, Cindy. It's a big one, the kind that might need a crusading journalist to handle. I hope you're up to it." Listening to myself saying this, it sounded lame, but what other option did we have? If the editor had been some macho guy I would have sent Maya in to pitch it. She could ratchet up the charm and was expert in the uses of cleavage.

"Try me." Cindy looked at me as if I were Deep Throat.

"The Vergruen Reference Collection. What do you think? It's a cultural story with a sinister twist." I gave her my best cub reporter smile.

"Page five, it's a snooze, Paul. Two inches of free publicity below the fold. We've already done it and nobody cares about fakes anyway. Besides, it closes on the weekend. It's history. What else have you got? Come on, get my blood going. It needs a boost today; it's all collecting down in my ankles."

"You used their press release for your story, right?"

"With suitable embellishments. We don't just *copy*

it." A trace of indignation.

"What I'm going to tell you wasn't in your story. It's not the kind of publicity they were looking for."

"So what did I miss? You want me to do an exposé on fake art? I was hoping you were going to tell me you'd killed someone again and the police didn't know it yet. An exclusive. I can see the headline: *'Police Helpless as Zacher Strikes Again in New Wave of Mayhem.'*"

"It could happen, but we're not that far into the case yet. Let me tell you the story."

"Can I quote you?"

"Why not?" She switched on her tape recorder. I was probably going to regret this, but I couldn't resist running my name past Glass again now that we were going to take him on. I'm not that full of myself, but I didn't care for the pompous way he had dismissed me. So I gave Cindy the entire thing anyway, starting with my first visit to the VRC show. Even the part about the billiard cue in St. Jerome's hand in my own version, which she said was a good human-interest angle.

When I finished, she said, "*'Local Painter Exposes Major Art Heist.'* I like it. We ditch the fact that you're also a detective, and make it an all-art story."

"You can point up the fact that as an artist, I see things differently. Can it make Friday's edition?"

"By a hair, but my old headline was *'Possible Frost on Saturday in Low-lying Areas,'* without much text below. I won't miss it. When you're down to the weather you know you're in trouble. People buy headlines, even here."

"Let me ask you something. Do you run a galley proof or anything like that before you start the print run?"

"Sure, the printer does, for proofreading."

"When is that available?"

"That would be Thursday about noon. Then I have time to make corrections before we go to press that night."

"Would it be possible to get a copy of the front page so I could fax it to someone back home?"

"Sure. Your parents?"

"Something like that. Actually, an old professor of mine from art school. He'll be surprised to see how well I've done for myself. I'll stop by and pick it up."

It looked like the timing of this would be about right. Glass might have enough time to set up the disappearance of the six paintings, probably as the exhibit was being dismantled and packed. We'd be ready for him. It felt good to be ahead of the curve for once on a case, calling the shots, but it also made me wonder if I was getting ahead of myself.

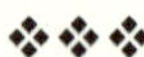

On Thursday at lunchtime I called Glass's Texas office and got his fax number from the secretary. I realized it didn't matter now if he recognized my full name or not from the newspaper interview; he'd be coming after me no matter who I was. Back at home after calling on Cindy, I cut the galley into letterhead-size sections and fed them into the fax. I wondered briefly whether we should involve Delgado, but decided against it. The additional firepower he could provide might be useful, but I wanted to take possession of the pictures myself. It could be the beginning of the Zacher Reference Collection, if only briefly. Its mission could be to educate museum directors on how to recognize the real thing after it disappeared from their collections. I wasn't up on the latest auction results, but I estimated the value of the remaining six at between $30 and $40 million.

As I got out my gun and cleaned it, I wondered how the VRC had slipped to this miserable low point. The story of Piet Vergruen was well known, and he had operated from the highest motives. After the initial shock from the appraisal, it had never shamed him that he inherited the original fakes from his father, and he apparently didn't think it shamed his father either. His purpose had been to educate people to keep them from being victimized as his family had been. After a few years at it, he must have known the art world was full of people who needed his help. Many museum curators and private collectors had an art historian's background like Glass did, and they wouldn't be able to look at art the way a painter could.

And how had Glass gotten control of the VRC? Naturally most museum administrators wouldn't want the job of sponsoring exhibitions of fakes all over the world. For most of them it would have been an obvious drop in status, even though the travel perks were good. The chairman of a medium-sized college art department in Ohio might have been as good as the Vergruen could get on the limited budget of its endowment. I wondered how long it had taken him to sense the possibilities. Probably even before he signed the employment contract.

As I was feeding rounds into the cylinder of my .38, the doorbell rang and I let Cody in.

"Did you get the fax off?" he said.

"It's gone. I wish I could have seen Glass's face."

"They'll wait until Sunday, then, when they're taking down the show. No point in staging another break-in when they have to take all the pictures away anyway. What I think will happen is that the six won't ever show up back at their warehouse, and nobody will say a word. Because they deal in fakes, this outfit has no accountability."

"I'm wondering now if we even needed the newspaper article," I said. "We could have stolen the pictures anyway."

"But this way they know who did it. They'll come out of the woodwork again, and that will bring Glass back down here. If the pictures get back to Baker Falls and they're stashed where no one can find them, what kind of a case do we have? No expert can testify about them."

"True, but Maya's not going to enjoy wearing a target again," I said.

"She's doing OK. She knew how it would be when she came back to the Zacher Agency." This understated what had happened; Maya had left me and gone back to México City for several months last year, knowing that I was into the detective business too deeply to back out. She returned because she'd convinced herself she could manage the risk better if she were in charge. This situation might severely test that assumption, since we didn't know what resources Glass had behind him.

"You haven't said anything to Delgado, have you?" said Cody.

"No, because I want the pictures. If we pull him into this now, he's going to take them, if he believes what I say about them. If not, he'll just return them to the VRC and ask me to explain why I shouldn't be in jail for grand theft. I'm not sure I could." Felony grand theft here is stealing anything more than five tortillas at once.

"Why do I think you just want to hang them in your studio and gloat?"

"I don't know," I said. "Why *do* you?"

"Just an old cop's hunch. Think of the security you'd need."

"We're all going to need it when Glass finds out we've taken them."

"What if we kill some of the crew and Delgado still doesn't believe the paintings are real?"

"I'm betting that the slugs they recovered from Ortíz's head match one of their guns," I said. "That'll be enough."

"I wonder if we should start surveillance Saturday night? A normal crew would wait until Sunday, or even Monday, but these guys are probably special. Nonunion, I think. No problem with odd hours, and they might see the cover of darkness as a plus."

"The show closes at nine."

"We'll be there."

CHAPTER 5
DR. BERNHARD GLASS

Dr. Bernhard Glass, although a fourth generation American from the Midwest, had distinctly Anglophile tastes. His principal office was in Texas because that was where the previous director had lived and the VRC was warehoused, but Glass preferred working from London whenever possible, thinking that a European location buttressed his expertise. While at one level he didn't believe it required any validation, at the same time, he presided over a collection of fakes, and he didn't like being thought of as having less status than the director of any other collection of classic paintings. After all, some of his fakes were nearly 200 years old and, after deceiving that many people for that long, deserved their own kind of respect.

Fifty-nine years old, Glass was a wide man of florid complexion. He sometimes thought, as he leaned into the bathroom mirror inspecting his teeth, that his fleshy build suggested a heart attack lurked down the road, but he enjoyed his lifestyle too much to change it. He was partial to subtly pinstriped Saville Row suits and custom-made shoes. His trademark bow ties were bespoke too. In Mayfair, his townhouse was graced by a rotating assortment from the Vergruen holdings, displayed against

1820s Regency paneling that subtly attested to their genuineness. In some cases this was unnecessary, because he enjoyed hanging stolen pictures as well as fakes. Invariably, when they weren't stolen, the others were the finest examples of the forger's trade, enough to make visiting curators nearly weep with envy, even though they thought they knew what they were looking at. It also made them wonder whether some of the stars of their own museum collections should be hung there too.

It was not lost on Glass that London was also the original home of the VRC. To him, this provided an attractive symmetry. As he sat in his study on an early Thursday evening, he was fantasizing over the catalogue of a recent show at the Metropolitan Museum in New York, wondering whether he might be able to make off with one of their Vermeers at some point. He had every confidence that Natty Bollander was up to it. Although the man had the creativity of a greeter at Walmart, Glass knew he was a technical genius of the highest rank.

Without success Dr. Glass tried not to watch his fax machine spitting out a particularly noxious newspaper report about seven genuine paintings being discovered in the nearly finished show in a hick town in México—one he now regretted having ever heard of. If hadn't been a slow spot in the season, he never would have put VRC paintings at risk there. According to the story, the seven included the la Tour that had been previously stolen from the show. His secretary in Baker Falls had forwarded the clippings without comment, but he knew she must have read them. She would bear watching more closely in the future.

He recognized the name Paul Zacher as the

nervy painter and pseudo-expert who had called on him a couple weeks earlier, an event that had prompted him to have the Georges de la Tour removed from the Bellas Artes in San Miguel. But Zacher's name meant nothing to him beyond that. Glass's days as an art department chairman occupied a rear space in the file cabinet drawer of his memory. With the appearance of this additional affront he wished now that he'd ordered all the real pictures taken down at the same time as the la Tour was "stolen." But he hadn't been able to convince himself that Zacher could have recognized the others. What would a mere painter know? A deep flush covered Glass's face as he finished reading the third page and then slapped the papers down on his desktop next to the catalogue.

He didn't recognize the name *Atención*, but any publicity was unacceptable, even from some two bit local paper in a nowhere town in México. A story could always be picked up and sent out on the wire services in the States. Or it might appear on some busybody's art blog, run as an amusement by someone with no more savvy than Paul Zacher. The idea that even a single one of the Vergruen Reference Collection pictures could be genuine was a deadly blot on its reputation, which he now identified completely with his own. It was his expertise, coupled with that reputation, that now and for some time had validated his life.

Ironically, some people require the shadow of past adversity to illuminate their achievements, illustrating that their upward course has not been smooth, in the same way that a painter adds contrasting darks next to highlights to boost their impact in a picture. It was like mascara. For Bernhard Glass this contrast was provided by the dense shadow of his humble beginnings.

His father had been a manufacturer's rep in men's sportswear, his mother, a tenth grade dropout who had worked as a maid in a wealthy household in Cleveland. Of course, they hadn't understood his desire for college, which they correctly saw more as a need to become what they had never been and had never felt the need to become. Their only son was a climber, eager to leave them behind. In Glass's view, their failure to grasp their own shortcomings had in itself been their greatest shortcoming. He had been aware of this from an early age.

Bernhard Glass had no offspring. Instead, he had nurtured his career as he would an only child, lavishing endless hours and care on each advancement, pausing only to sample here and there the charms of certain college girls who suggested to him the lithe figures so favored by Sandro Botticelli; tall willowy girls with small breasts and red or reddish blond hair. Their milky skin and innocent but inviting faces with rosebud lips lingered in his dreams even after they had moved on. Often they tended to be of Irish extraction. Some had delightfully pre-Raphaelite features.

He had firmly kept his wife in the background during his rise through the faculty ranks. She was the only serious mistake of his life, one he was determined never to repeat. When she had wearied of his emotional absence and naively taken up with a notorious womanizer, he had signed the divorce decree with no regret. He knew from the way she had fanatically kept the affair secret long after she was free and able to do anything she wanted, that it had begun considerably before their marriage ended. Her sense of guilt was clearly visible, even draped in her current mantle of moral superiority, which had gone on for years. They no longer communicated, a condition that had effectively begun before the marriage ended, but was now official. Glass enforced it ruthlessly.

He reached for the phone and dialed Collin Welch, who headed his installation crew. Welch was also charged with engineering the substitutions that provided Glass with genuine old masters. After a suitable period on exhibit as fakes, they were quietly sold in Switzerland through a broker whose discretion was legendary. By this process, Glass had amassed a fortune nearly as large as the VRC endowment; his $125,000 a year salary barely covered his fine wines and cigars, and the quarterly pairs of bespoke shoes.

"Where are you now?" he said, when Welch answered.

"We got into San Miguel last night. We're about to take down the show. What's happening?"

"We're going to have to segregate those other six pictures, you know the ones I mean. When you get them back across the border, put them in storage at Dillon's. We can't show them again anywhere."

"No problem. Did someone spot them?"

"A painter down there named Paul Zacher. It's possible he might still be a problem."

"What kind of problem?"

"I'm not sure. Maybe nothing, but be careful. If he makes any attempt to interfere when you're loading, I want you to deal with it. Take him out if you have to, do you understand? Make sure the others are armed."

"Of course. What's he got against you, Dr. Glass? You're a patron of the arts."

"I can't imagine. He's probably only trying to prove something. I really hesitate to eliminate anyone else down there, but if he shows up and you can't see another way to immobilize him, then do it. But don't just drop him on the side of the road like you did with Ortíz, put him in a place where he won't be found. Like maybe he left town for a while. I don't want a lot of noise about it. We've already had some unfortunate publicity."

"What if the police connect the dots?"

"Those Méxican cops? Probably nothing, but it can't be helped at this point. I've already got buyers lined up for five of those pictures. Bring this off without a hitch and there's a bonus in it for you."

"Consider it done, Dr. Glass."

Glass could almost see him salute. After he hung up, the director leaned back in his chair and pressed his palms together, now slightly moist with an unwelcome anxiety. Perhaps his policy of concealing stolen paintings by hanging them in VRC shows was not a good idea after all, although it was a brilliant way of moving them around without triggering any scrutiny. A gray fog crept up against the windows of his study, obscuring the traffic below. He didn't relish the fact that murder had now been required to keep his game afloat, and would possibly be again, but as they said in London, in for a penny, in for a pound. More than one, in this case. The seven pictures he had inserted into the México show represented his biggest take so far, and while using his Swiss broker to liquidate them would result in a discount to auction prices, they were stolen and full retail was impossible. Still, he was expecting to walk away with $15 million after the broker's commission, as much as his salary for 112 years.

CHAPTER 6

At 8:45 on Saturday night we wandered through the exhibition one last time to verify that our prey was still in place. I could see Maya wasn't happy, but she hadn't made any objections. She'd worn her bottle-green blazer over jeans and a pale blue work shirt, and her hair was tied back. She'd left her jewelry at home. The paintings were all still there, and I examined the six individually, checking for any more substitutions. Leaving, she paused outside the Bellas Artes.

"It'll be alright," she said. "We'll be up to it." I gave her a quick hug, but I thought I saw doubt lingering in her eyes. We retired to the Town and Country, all in the rear seats behind the black glass. Precisely at nine o'clock, seven people emerged from the Bellas Artes and the guard locked the door. Then nothing more happened for two hours. I was beginning to wonder whether this made any sense, when two unlabeled box vans pulled up onto the staging area before the door on Hernandez Macias. No one got out. Five minutes later an anonymous Ford van with no windows in the back or sides pulled up behind the other two. Four doors opened as if on cue and six men got out, looking up and down the street.

"I don't like the odds here," said Maya, but then, she never did. She unbuttoned her blazer to make her gun more accessible. We probably could have had the México can army bivouacked behind us and she wouldn't have felt much better.

A tall, slender man from the Ford unlocked the door of the Bellas Artes and went inside. I thought it was interesting that these anonymous people had keys to one of our major cultural institutions. Four of the others followed, and from their demeanor they were expecting something. I was sure Glass must have warned them. The sixth man stood leaning against the driver's side door of the Ford van, watching the street. We were illegally parked on the other side, down about fifty feet, near the Mesones intersection, alongside the Angela Peralta Theater.

"They've made their first mistake," said Cody, "leaving just one guy out there. Never leave a man alone when you don't know what's coming at him. Maya, here comes your part. They won't be expecting an attractive Méxican woman. Slip out on the curb side and cross Hernandez Macias further down by the entrance to Bacco. When you walk back up the sidewalk on their side, come around the front of the Ford and point your gun at him. He won't have time to get his out. Then bring him over here."

He reached onto the dash and dialed the interior lights down to nothing. Maya silently opened the front door, not saying a word, leaving it open a few inches. The man glanced at her briefly as she crossed the street down past the Tio Lucas Restaurant, then looked the other way. She obviously represented no threat. I pulled out my gun and watched the Bellas Artes door in case anyone came back out to the loading area during Maya's approach.

"I know what you're thinking," Cody said, as we

waited, "but we need her for this. If either of us came up to that guy on the street, he'd have his gun out and then we'd have to kill him. The others would hear the shot and would come out. We're going to need someone left alive on their side to talk to us."

I didn't like it, but I could see his logic. I also knew he wouldn't put Maya at risk unnecessarily; he'd rather see me take a bullet.

Sensing a threat, the man turned suddenly as she moved quickly across the front of the Ford with her gun aimed at his chest. She knew better than to aim at his head; heads move too fast and present a smaller target than a chest. He raised his hands slowly, and she gestured in our direction.

"Hurry," I whispered. "Hurry up now. Get him over here."

She moved him across the street, staying out of his reach two steps behind, and soon they were out of sight of the Bellas Artes door behind a tour van parked behind us. We got out, guns leveled, and slid open our side door. I collected the man's gun and tied his hands behind his back while Cody shoved a rag in his mouth. He was obviously an American. It made me think that Glass didn't have anyone on the ground in San Miguel. We pushed him inside and tied his ankles.

"One down." We got back in the van and waited. Two minutes later another man came out carrying a box I assumed contained a painting and stopped uneasily at the side of the Ford. He leaned it against the rear doors and walked around the van looking for the first man. When he realized he was alone, he picked up the picture and ran back inside with it.

"Shit," I said, but I didn't know how else it could have gone. The only way to avoid a drawn-out battle was to pick them off one by one.

Immediately four men came out and separated, guns drawn, looking up and down the street. One of them said something over his shoulder and the door opened again and the man with the painting returned to the Ford van, sliding it inside the back door while the others covered him. Ten good-looking Méxican women wouldn't have any effect on them now.

"What's next?" I asked.

"We just let them load, I think. Nothing else we can do," said Cody.

The same man brought out five more boxed pictures, one at a time, and loaded them. The five men held a conference at the front of the Ford, and then two got in and backed it up. We did nothing. The van pulled out and moved down Hernandez Macias toward Canal, and after a moment one of the men went back in. The other two stayed to watch the street.

I waited until they looked in the other direction and then started the engine and pulled into the street. I drove casually at first, but I was afraid the van with the stolen art would get away, so I hit the accelerator as we passed the Bellas Artes entrance. They got off two shots before I turned on Canal, one of which sounded like it glanced off the top edge in back, and then we were too far away. So much for my flawless new van.

"They're not going to be chasing us in one of those big trucks," said Maya, with some relief as she got up off the floor, brushing the dust off her hands. "We should vacuum this again."

With no one behind us, we sped down Canal, and went left on Zacateros in the direction of Ancha de San Antonio. About a block ahead I could see the Ford, driving on the normal side of fast, but not enough to draw attention. With his cargo, he still had to slow for speed bumps. Little other traffic appeared as he passed the long stone façade of the Instituto. I kept back some distance, but not to stay anonymous. I assumed that someone from the trucks would have called the van and told them about us. This looked like it could end badly; nothing new there.

"Stay back a bit more," said Cody. "One of them is leaning out the passenger side. I can't see if he's got his gun out, but he probably has."

At the Cardo intersection, a pickup suddenly pulled directly in front of us and I slammed on the brakes just inches from hitting it. He didn't move. I paused a second to clear my head from the shock and was just starting to open my door when I saw a rapid movement in my side mirror and felt a gun pressed to my ear. From the corner of my eye I saw another man covering Cody on the passenger side. I glanced back in the rear view mirror as Maya put her hands on top of her head. I couldn't see her face from the rear view mirror, but that was fine. I knew what it looked like.

"Give me your keys and your gun," said the man next to me. They were both Americans. I handed the gun to him slowly and the other man collected Maya's and Cody's guns and the keys to the van, then slid open the side door. Behind us waited a white Suburban, inches from our rear bumper. The man pulled Maya out and shoved her into the Suburban while the second man cut the ropes on our prisoner and he followed them back, tossing his gag on the street. With tires squealing, the pickup and the Suburban both sped away. It had taken less than a minute. I got the license number of the Suburban but not the pickup. The Ford van we'd been chasing was out of sight. Cody pounded the Town and Country with both fists, screaming obscenities. We ran back to my house on Quebrada and collected my spare van key, but when we returned to the intersection where we'd left it, it was gone. Normally the Transito police aren't that quick. Too late we realized we should have left Cody with it. There's no good manual on how to do this stuff.

Cody stayed with me that night. Neither of us could sleep, so we sat in the great room with a pot of coffee and went over what had happened.

"It's rule six of the fundamental principles of police work, that's where we blew it," he said, drawing on his snifter of cognac to brace up the coffee. "Never assume you know how many you're going up against. As we watched them working, it seemed to me that six of them was about right. Besides, we were focused on the Ford van with the real paintings when I should have been watching our backs. I could have held them off as they got out of the car. Now she's gone." His voice cracked, and he put both hands over his face, rubbing hard. When he took them away again, his eyes were wet.

We had gotten Delgado out of bed as soon as we got to my place. I gave him the license number of the Suburban and a description of the other vehicles. He said he was on it but we heard nothing more until six A.M. He called back then to say my van had been found and towed and could be picked up at the impound lot on the Querétaro road next to the police horse barn. The police had not found any of the other vehicles. Cody pocketed my extra keys and took a cab out to get it while I waited by the phone to hear from—or about—Maya.

After he left, I sat there wondering how long it was going to take for us to get this right, and what getting it wrong this time was going to cost Maya. But for the need to handle this in a rational manner, Cody and I would both have been screaming long ago.

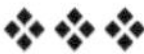

For an endless three days that felt like a month, we heard nothing. When Maya left me for three months last year, at least then I knew she was safe, even if in someone else's arms, briefly. This was a new level of torture. I called Delgado every morning and afternoon, listening to his apologies. They were genuine and heartfelt, but always much the same. He made no excuses. No trace of either the Suburban or the pickup had been found, and no information extracted from the three remaining workers loading the VRC show, who simply denied there had ever been a sixth member of their crew. Delgado had found nothing to charge them with; they were employees doing the job they'd been hired for. While this can sometimes be unusual in México, it's not a crime. He'd found no trace of the Ford van with the genuine paintings, and, of course, no trace of Maya.

"Couldn't the men in the van have been stopped at the border, if they were headed for the States?" I'd asked Delgado during our first conversation.

"Of course they could have been." Here he shrugged, as if to say, why would you expect this? "We forwarded information to all the checkpoints. But they weren't stopped. I suspect that they had a large supply of cash with them. Or perhaps they haven't left México." Either way, they'd have had a struggling Méxican woman under a tarp in the back. Or, ironically, perhaps they had slipped her over the fence somewhere in the Sonoran desert like an illegal farm worker. Being from a good family of the professional class, that means of entry would have made her angrier than the kidnapping.

I hadn't gone out, even for food, waiting for a call. Cody went to Mega for groceries, and kept company with me afterward, at least as angry and frustrated as I was. I was certain they weren't going to ask for a ransom, even if they had known about the $700,000 I still had from a phony inheritance paid me during the Malcolm Brendel case to make it look like I had a motive for killing him. Naturally I'd kept it—at least now we had the resources to deal with whatever came up. But I knew this wasn't about money; it was about keeping us at bay while they concealed the stolen paintings.

Cody was still with me on the evening of the third day when the phone finally rang.

But it was not Bernhard Glass or any of his fake-loving associates on the other end. It was a tentative-sounding woman who identified herself as Sheila Roper.

"Is this Paul Zacher?"

"Yes." It wasn't the call I wanted, and I knew I sounded impatient.

"You don't know me, but I found your name in *Juarde*."

Juarde is the phonebook for San Miguel's expatriate community, the word itself a pun on *Who Are They*, but spelled and pronounced as if it were a Spanish word.

"We're not taking any new cases at the moment," I said. "We've got our hands full."

"I know, but this is about the case you're working on, the kidnapping and art theft. I think I can help you."

"How is that?"

"I'd rather not say on the phone. It would be better if I could see you. Can I come over? I know where you live." This last sentence was one I'd heard before on other cases, but this time it didn't cause my blood to run cold as I ran to bolt the door. Cody was making impatient gestures. My first reaction was skepticism, but we had no other leads, not that I thought this could be one.

"All right," I said.

"I'll be there in ten minutes."

I hung up and, with a shrug, gave Cody the details.

"Ever heard of her?"

"No. Not that it means anything. She says she just wants to help."

"Help who, I wonder?"

"What do you mean?" I said.

"I've run into this before, more than once. Some people out there prey on the families of murder and kidnap victims. They're like emotional vampires."

"How would she know about Maya being kidnapped? I'm so stressed I didn't even realize that when she said it. The only information in the paper was about the stolen paintings."

"Well, she's gotten it somewhere. Maybe she

knows someone in Delgado's office. Even if she isn't involved, some people get a thrill from being close to a crime like this. In knowing the victim's family, they get to experience the grief second hand; they almost get to touch you. They feed off your reaction to tragedy. It's a way of feeling something intense."

"Ghoulish, I'd say. So, what they really need is to get a life?"

"Pretty much. Their own emotional range has flat-lined."

I went into the kitchen and mixed us a couple of margaritas. I had just set them down on the table in the loggia when the doorbell rang. When I opened the door I saw a woman in a straight black skirt and a pale green silk blouse topped with a French blue scarf loosely knotted at her neck. She looked moderately over forty, with a youthful expression, rather tentative. Sheila Roper had shoulder-length dark hair and wore no jewelry. Coming in, she offered her hand to me. I thought she was attractive without being devastating, but maybe I was already devastated enough by Maya's kidnapping.

"Come in," I said. "Join us for a drink in the garden." I bolted the door firmly behind her. She nodded with a vague smile and followed me out to the *loggia*. I had turned on the ground lights among the plantings so she could get a better sense of her surroundings. We could see all the way back into the bamboo on the rear wall. The fountain was bubbling. "This is my associate, Cody Williams."

Cody rose and shook her hand as I went back inside to make her a drink. I couldn't imagine how she thought she could help us, but maybe she'd seen something the night Maya was kidnapped.

"—Agency," she was saying as I returned with her margarita. "We book tours throughout Latin America, but mostly México, and some Caribbean cruises, of course."

"Do you enjoy that?" asked Cody, looking at her appraisingly, obviously still curious about the reason for her visit. He was not wearing his toughest look, which at this stage would have been more opaque than skeptical. I assumed he reserved that for men he didn't trust. Shelia Roper was sitting upright in her chair, as if being quizzed.

"Very much. I seem to have a knack for sensing what people like to do on vacation." She turned to me as I set her margarita down. Sheila Roper was starting to look more relaxed, and I felt a modest warmth coming off her.

"What kind of information do you have?" I asked, sitting down opposite her. Normally I try to be more subtle than this, but I was heavily stressed and still hoping the phone would ring at any moment.

She hesitated a moment. "It's sort of vague, really, just a feeling. I should explain something. I often get impressions about things; from out of the blue, I mean. Maybe I have a kind of antenna that picks up information: feelings, sensations, often it's no more than ordinary facts. Am I making any sense?"

"Go on." She wasn't, but I was hoping for something more. I glanced at Cody, who was wearing his cop mask with a slightly encouraging smile, but still giving nothing away. I saw a crinkle around his eyes, and I suddenly realized that he liked this woman. He was responding to her, although she represented the opposite of what drove him—factual information.

"I had this feeling," she went on, "about a kidnapping being connected to the art theft at the Bellas Artes, and I had a sudden image of your girlfriend. She's in a room with a heat source. Maybe it's a furnace or an oven, I can't see it well, but the place feels warm and humid. I don't see any windows. It could even be a bakery. The details I get are often sketchy. She's not tied up, though, so she's free to move around."

"Any idea where this might be?"

"Not at this point, but sometimes I get more if I'm thinking about it a lot, but only indirectly. Like when it's hanging about at the back of my mind, and I'm not trying to force it."

I looked at her more closely now. She had a dark complexion that went well with her hair, and her eyes held a hopeful but tentative look, as if her gift was not always well received, even when it gave a true account, at least as she could see it. Her insights probably put her in a tough spot sometimes, since they could rarely be verified.

"What was she wearing?" asked Cody in an unthreatening tone, placidly placing one meaty hand over the other on the table. His expression said he regarded her remarks with interest, and although he was open to listening, it was going to take a little more to convince him.

Sheila's brown eyes looked back at him calmly. Being questioned on detail was obviously nothing new to her. "It's a jacket, cut like a blazer, green. Dark pants, possibly jeans? Light shirt, blue I think, like a work shirt."

I couldn't prevent a chill from coming over me at this point, but then I thought she must have talked to someone who saw the kidnapping happen, or she had seen us earlier waiting in front of the Bellas Artes before the paintings came out. However, Delgado had been unable to find any witnesses on the street. Canal at that point is mostly commercial, and aside from a couple of restaurants, the shops had closed for the day not long after we parked. San Antonio was carrying almost no traffic when we lost Maya. Maybe Delgado hadn't located anyone, but Sheila Roper might have.

"Can I take your hand?" she went on. Before I could move it out of the way she grasped it in both of hers, prying it open palm upward. "I can tell you don't believe me, do you? It's all right. But I think you'd like to. I can tell you something else, too. She didn't want to go with you two the night that she was kidnapped. She thought you might be wrong about what was happening. And also, you don't think this is about a ransom." No witness could have told her these things. She was right. I did not want to believe her, but...

"Didn't you ever have an experience like that where you suddenly knew something that you couldn't have known?" she went on. "It's not only me, I think everybody does. Maybe not as often as people like me, but it still happens a lot. The difference is that most people want to ignore it. I don't. I've learned to trust it."

As she said this, something came back to me instantly, although I hadn't thought of it since high school. "In math class I used to know in advance the number the teacher was about to say. It didn't happen all the time, and it wasn't ever the answer to some problem he'd given us that I could have solved before he said it. There was never any context that would suggest it. The numbers just popped into my head before he said them."

"That's exactly what I mean. How about you,

Cody?" She was now moderating a class in ESP, looking for volunteers whose experience would reinforce her position. I could see he was struggling with this as she got stronger. She touched the hairy back of his hand with a single finger, and then he brightened as if she'd set something in motion.

"For me, I've often had the false recognition thing. It still happens once a year or so, although it used to be more often. I'll be walking down the street, any street, and I'll see someone I haven't connected with in a long time and wouldn't expect to run into. Then, as I get closer, I realize I was mistaken. The person ahead of me only resembles the one I thought I saw."

"I don't think that's what she's talking about," I said.

"But wait. Then, only three or four blocks later, I actually *do* see the person I was just thinking that I saw. I've never understood it. Are you telling me that's what this is like?"

"Right." Sheila's look said he could easily be her most promising student. "It jumps into your head uninvited and out of context. It's always a surprise. That's how it happens to me. The images I get don't even have to be about someone I know. In fact, they're usually about total strangers."

"How does that connect with your psychology background?" I asked Cody. I felt like this was getting farther into New Age territory than I was comfortable with.

"Oh, this thing is out there, alright." He was nodding, but the look on his face was less than comfortable. "Usually when researchers try to test for it, the results are so inconsistent that they get a statistically insignificant outcome. They can be all over the map. Someone makes a connection with something they couldn't have known in a million years, and then can never repeat it. Science doesn't appreciate those kinds of results. I can't recall that anyone has ever proved conclusively that it really exists. But I did see it happen once on the force. A woman came in, and now that I say that, I wonder if they aren't mostly women who can do this? Anyway, she said she knew where the body of a missing schoolgirl was. It had come to her out of nowhere, and she was right. She had no connection with the case and she couldn't have known what we might find. We hadn't even been sure the girl was dead."

"And then she told you who killed her," I said.

"No. She couldn't come up with that part, and the case was never solved. She said she couldn't make it happen when she wanted to. That was all she was ever able to give us. At least the parents got closure, but the police never did."

"That's the way it is with me, too," Sheila said. "I can't make myself do it. It started when I was a kid. The first time it happened, I told my mother, and it made her really uncomfortable, so I didn't mention it to her again."

"But you touched my hand and then told me more," I said.

"I know. If I can touch a person, it comes more easily, but still not usually on demand."

"Another one?" I asked, noticing that her glass was empty. Cody and I were still working on ours.

"Please." Sheila paused, turning toward me as I moved away to the kitchen. "Your friend traveled a long way, Paul. It was mostly in the dark."

"Is she alright now?" I paused in the doorway, not

breathing. I didn't know whether I should believe what she was about to say or not.

"I don't know. Sorry, but I usually can't answer any questions. I draw a blank when I try. It's not that I don't want to. You've taken me more seriously than most people do."

"Have you ever worked with the police here?" asked Cody. I left the swinging door to the kitchen open so I could listen.

"I tried once. About two years ago I contacted an investigator named Licenciado Segun about something that came to me. I saw a man from the Yucatan being shot in the head up by the Charco. Segun wasn't interested in hearing what I had to say."

Cody gave me a covert look as I stood at the counter inside. This sounded like part of our first case. "What did Segun say?"

"He said, no thank you. That the police had their own method of solving cases, and dreams or visions weren't part of it. I thought he was pretending not to understand it, because it wasn't a dream I'd had. I made that clear, but he still didn't want to hear about it. Not the first time I'd had that response, so I didn't push it, and I just went away. Usually no one offers me a margarita, either. I feel like I've helped a little here." She ended with a broad smile, and said no more. At a different time of the year we would have heard crickets in the garden. Now there was only grim silence as we thought about what she'd said.

"Interesting scarf." I set her drink on the table. While some women would have taken it off and showed it to me, Sheila pulled it tighter under her chin.

"I always wear one, I have a scar on my neck."

"A dog attacked you?" Now it was spreading; Cody had become psychic too.

"Not bad! It happened when I was seven. I knew he was going to. That's what I told my mother that upset her. She said I had caused it myself, that I must have been teasing him, and that's how I knew it would happen. But I hadn't done anything to him. A nasty vibe was coming off him as I walked by."

"Have you had any training since you discovered this gift, a process that might help you focus it better, and perhaps get results more consciously or consistently?" I asked.

"No. Maybe I should try that. There are people I could talk to here, but I don't know that it would help, though, because it comes from a different part of my brain. A door that's closed most of the time."

"Does a drink or two open it up?" I asked.

"No, that's just for fun, but I'm glad you don't think I'm handing you some line. Or do you?" A minute wrinkle formed on her forehead.

"Let me answer that with another question," said Cody. The old cop trick. "What do you expect to get from this? What do you see as your role in this investigation?" I could see he was still warming to her, but this was a question he felt he had to ask.

Sheila raised her hands as if in self-defense.

"Nothing, really, Cody. I only wanted to help. Actually, I *hate* approaching people with information; I usually get the strangest responses. I've learned to keep my mouth shut when it's bad news, and it often is. In this case, I thought it would be good news because I sensed that you didn't have much. Once, I noticed a couple walking toward me down the street and I saw the man with another woman, holding hands with her while he had his other arm through his wife's. I knew right away he had a girlfriend. I could see her perfectly. I understood because she made his wife look like a dog. Naturally I walked on past without saying anything. Usually it's none of my business anyway."

"I can see that," said Cody, with a smile. His eyes were scanning the detail of her face.

Later, Sheila got onto some stories about the travel business, one in particular about a couple she'd booked on a Caribbean cruise where the wife had taken up with one of the stewards and the husband threatened to sue the travel company and the cruise line. The lawyer he'd hired told him that since the cruise had been purchased in México, any such behavior on the part of his wife would be considered fate, and not actionable, except by God, and that would only come later. The courts could take no part in it.

At about 10:30 I called a cab for Sheila Roper. She thanked us profusely for the hospitality, promising to share any other insights she had with us. She even had a sentimental moment as she got into the cab, as if she'd joined our efforts in a significant way. I didn't discourage this idea. I got the feeling that her input was rarely as welcome as it had been that night. Her last words to us were, "I'll be following you. Don't worry." I had given her my cell phone number.

Cody took the ID number of the vehicle and told the driver in an authoritative voice that he was responsible for getting her home with no incidents. Normally we would have driven her home ourselves, but we were still tied to the phone, waiting for word from Maya. I went back to the *loggia* to finish cleaning up.

"She likes to talk," said Cody.

"Some women don't get out much. I imagine her gift is as much of a problem as a benefit to people she's never met. I applaud her for taking a chance with us."

"Maybe she thought we were more vulnerable than most."

"Yet, she would've had to really see something about the case to come up with that much information."

"The two margaritas loosened her up." Cody said. With Cody's build, even the way I make them, I've never seen margaritas cause the slightest tremor in his poise, except for the evening when I told him Maya had left me, and that wasn't entirely the margaritas.

"Do you think Sheila's legit?" I emphasized that last word.

"That's a tough read, yet I liked her more than I expected to. Look at each piece of her information, and collectively it could add up to no more than a combination of things she heard, plus a few shrewd guesses, things we can't verify."

"I think we need her, though," I said. "As much as I hate to be dependent on that kind of unpredictable process."

"But you liked her too, I could see that. Thin as it is, at this point she's all we've got. I think she's a keeper."

"I wish we'd thought to get her address."

"I have a feeling she'll find us again." It was not an example of clairvoyance, but Cody was right.

CHAPTER 7
DR. BERNHARD GLASS

Dr. Glass stood in the little-used back room of a dry cleaning store he owned in Baker Falls, Texas. It was three blocks from his office. The door leading to the unoccupied cleaning area was locked. The room he stood in normally contained only a steam generator and a small bathroom enclosed in one corner next to a storage locker for unclaimed clothing. Today it also held a cot and a prisoner of México nationality who was in the United States illegally, but not to pick grapes. However, had she been better armed, she would readily have picked a fight.

Glass had bought the business and the building three years earlier with proceeds from stolen picture sales. He'd always had his suits cleaned there when he was in the States and was impressed by the consistent job they did. It also proved to be a handy way to launder money, an irony that was not lost on him. As with his suits, the business did a superb job.

Now, as he stood looking at the woman, he could see she regarded him with extreme distaste. It didn't matter; not being a strawberry blond, she wasn't his type. He hadn't mentioned his name, but he thought she probably knew it already.

"I need some clean clothes," she said, "after all that time in the back of the truck." She was standing in one corner with her arms folded, keeping as far from him as possible.

Without responding, he unlocked the storage locker and pointed to rows of clean clothes on hangers, some folded on shelves below. "These are unclaimed," he said. "Take what you need, I'm sure you'll locate something that fits. You won't find any underwear, of course."

"I'll wait until you leave."

"I have no doubt you will."

Dr. Glass went out through the street door, locked it, and walked back up the street to his office. He harbored no ill feeling to the woman, but her value as a hostage was too great to ignore, even though the abduction had been improvised. She had the added value of taking Zacher out of the action without actually killing him. Collin Welch had duly been given his bonus. Meanwhile, Glass had to figure out a more secure place to keep her while he worked out his plan.

When Maya heard the lock turn behind him, she advanced to the storage locker and peeled off her blazer to expose her light blue work shirt, now wet through in places, clinging to the damp skin under her arms and above her breasts. Shuffling through the clothes, she found a white silk blouse in her size and a pair of green slacks that fit well except for being too short.

She folded her damp clothes and set them in a corner by the cot after she changed. A stack of hangers in the bottom of the locker caught her eye. She pulled one out and began to experiment. By closing the metal locker door she was able to insert the end of the hook portion of the thin hanger and bend it into different configurations. She had seen Cody picking locks many times, and she remembered the way some of the picks looked on the end, but she'd never tried it herself. Now she had plenty of time to study the problem, and about three dozen hangers to experiment with. The door to the street was an old one, with a lock that hadn't been updated in many years. If Glass had ever imagined the room as a holding cell, she thought, he would have installed better hardware.

Four hours later, with aching fingers and two broken nails, Maya walked up the sidewalk toward Dr. Glass's office. She had no money, no identification, no weapon, and no legal status, but she was in good shape; she had her freedom and her wits.

Out on the street, the air was only slightly less steamy than in the boiler room. Maya had no cell phone. It had stayed behind in her purse in San Miguel, and it was possible she wouldn't have service here anyway. She thought of flagging down a police car and telling her story, but it seemed to her that the word of an illegal Méxican in Texas wouldn't stand up against that of the head of a respected cultural institution.

The area where she found herself was on the northern edge of downtown, a street of modest storefronts and cheap hotels, with taller, but still modest, office buildings beginning a block or so farther on. She spotted a hardware store across the street and went in. A man behind the counter looked up at her and then went on ringing up a sale. At a display along one wall, Maya found an assortment of pocketknives mounted on hanging cards. She glanced back at the clerk to make sure he was occupied and then slipped a switchblade into her back pocket, regretting that she had left her blazer behind. A gun would have suited her purposes better, but she knew they were usually kept under lock and key. Back on the street, she waited for a few minutes in a doorway, watching the hardware store entrance, but no one emerged. She ripped the card away from the knife and threw it in a trash can, and with her back turned to the traffic, pressed the button and watched the five-inch blade dart from the handle, imagining it pressed against Glass's bulging neck.

Maya had first considered trying to get back across the border, but without a passport or any other ID, nothing would happen. While she occasionally still resented the risk that came with being part of the Zacher Agency, she'd never found herself incapable of action during a case. She would stay in the States and work it from that end.

She remembered the address of Glass's office because they had discussed on their earlier trip whether they all ought to go to see him. As she approached the building she had no plan. The main issue was how to get past the receptionist. On the fifth floor she found Glass's name on one of the doors, and moved back down the hall to wait by a water fountain. It was late morning. Maya felt that the receptionist had probably drunk coffee, and like everyone else, eventually she'd have to use the bathroom.

Half an hour later the woman emerged and moved down the hall in the opposite direction. Maya waited until the restroom door closed behind her before she entered the VRC office. As the switchblade snapped open she moved at a run through the inner door. Glass looked up with an expression of alarm on his face, his hands fluttering in panic as she approached. He began to rise, saying, "What the hell...?" but by then she was behind him, pulling him back down into his chair, and seizing his thick wiry hair in one hand as she pressed the blade to his throat. He slowly sat down, his hands outstretched before him, palms flat on the desk.

"OK," he said. "You're free now. What more do you want?"

"Pull out your gun and set in on the desk." She knew he had a gun because she'd seen it on his visit to the boiler room. He slowly pulled out his center drawer and lifted the automatic out by the barrel and set it near her on the desk. She released his hair and picked it up, sliding the safety to its off position and taking two steps back.

"Now get up. We're leaving. Head for the elevator. This gun will be on you the entire time. Don't think I won't use it—I've got some issues to settle with you, glasshole, and I'm ready. Just give me an excuse."

When the elevator arrived, no one else was using it. Once inside, she wiped her left hand on her pants leg, trying to get rid of the oil from his hair. She could still smell it.

"Stand by the buttons and press the one for the lobby." She moved to the opposite corner, watching him. "Where are the paintings, the real ones?"

"In a storage warehouse. Two blocks distant."

"Show me the way."

"And how do you propose to get them out of there?"

"Show them to me and you'll live. Give me your wallet and your cell phone, one at a time, then keep your hands behind you as we walk. If I don't see both of them I'll shoot you in the back; I know where your spine is. It'll sound like a Méxican car backfiring."

She slid his wallet and phone into her pockets and walked three paces behind Glass down the street. He didn't look back, and she didn't believe he could ever outrun her, even to save his life.

At the secured entry of a four-story brick warehouse, he unlocked the door. They took a freight elevator to the third floor, where he stopped before a cubicle near the end of the corridor and opened it, then paused.

"Go in," Maya said, "now."

When he stepped inside, she quickly counted the crated pictures and then struck him fiercely on the side of the head with the gun butt. He dropped heavily to the floor without even raising his hands, slamming his forehead on the planks. "Don't mess with the head of the Zacher Agency," she said quietly, as she removed the warehouse and cubicle keys from his pocket.

On the way in she'd seen several flatbed carts lined up against the wall. One of them had a coil of rope looped over the push bar. She cut off a length with her switchblade and tied Glass's hands and feet, then pulled his monogrammed linen handkerchief from his breast pocket and stuffed it in his mouth.

Out in the corridor she scanned the other cubicles and found five that were empty with no padlock. Picking the one farthest from Glass, she moved the seven paintings into it. They were all crated in heavy cardboard and labeled. When all seven were inside, she put Glass's padlock on the door and slipped the key into her pocket. Back in the original cubicle, Glass was still unconscious. He wouldn't be locked in, but he'd be disabled for a long time. She closed the door too firmly to be kicked open.

On the way out, Maya opened Glass's wallet and counted the money: $345. She jammed it into the pocket of her green pants and tossed the wallet into a trashcan by the elevator. Now she could afford lunch. She wouldn't mind a little Tex-Mex. Then she could see about going home.

CHAPTER 8

I had another call the next day around noon. Sheila Roper's voice was breathy and excited. "She's in a hardware store stealing a knife!"

"That doesn't sound at all like her." That was my first reaction, but maybe in this situation, it did. Maya didn't have any money. Her purse was still in my van when Cody picked it up at the impound lot, although her money had been removed.

"Where is she?"

"I couldn't tell, but it didn't look like México. It seemed like an American kind of store. She was looking at a display of all kinds of pocketknives. She glanced at the counter and then put one in her pocket. She was wearing a white blouse and green pants. Her hair was kind of a mess."

That didn't sound like Maya, either. It wasn't what she was wearing when she was kidnapped. How could she have bought a change of clothes with no money?

"Anything else?"

"No. That's all I saw. I hope it helps."

"Thanks," I said. "Anything helps." I hung up. Cody was pacing back and forth in the great room with a frustrated look.

"Sheila says Maya's gotten free and stolen a knife.

She has different clothes. Seems like she's in the States like we thought."

"She must be in Baker Falls. If she's free, and she's got a knife, she'll go after Glass. I wouldn't want to be him now."

I felt my stomach clench. "So we go up to Baker Falls, but how do we find her?"

"We could pull in their police." His face had a doubtful look. Cody had spent thirty years as the police. He knew them well.

"Right. To look for an illegal alien who just shoplifted a weapon and probably stabbed a museum curator to death, unless Sheila's full of *frijoles*. I'd say we don't want the cops within a mile of this if we ever hope to get her back."

"Sounds like our usual style—irregular, but occasionally effective. I'm OK with it."

Then the phone rang again. Sheila must have come up with more.

"Paul! Paul! It's me! I got loose," said Maya, her voice as clear as if she were down at the *jardín*. "Glass must have some kind of international cell service because I got through right away on his phone."

"On *his* phone? Thank God. I was going crazy thinking about what you might be going through." But at the back of my mind, I wasn't sure I wanted to know what her having his phone meant.

"Are you all right?"

"I'm fine."

"Did you, ah, have to kill Glass?"

"Of course not. I'm a guest here in the States, although I wanted to, and I could have. He's on ice, though. You and Cody can kill him later if you want. But I've got his gun and his money, and I stole one of those tricky knives where the blade shoots out when you press a button. You should see it. I just put it right on his neck and pulled his hair up and he gave me his gun without an argument."

I could visualize this with no difficulty.

"Are you still in Baker Falls?"

"Yes."

"Here, talk to Cody. He's pounding on my back."

"Wait, Paul. I've got the old master paintings too. All seven of them."

"Jesus, Maya! Do you even need us? Are you just calling in to say hello before you go off to the governor's ball in Austin?"

"Well somebody's got to get me back across the border, darling. I don't have my passport, and I'll need some help moving the pictures."

I handed Cody the phone and left the room as he erupted into explosions of joy. My hands were shaking as I found a Havana Monte Cristo and poured a cognac. Lighting it, I moved out to the garden. Twice in a five-minute period, all three of us had come within seconds of being killed on our last case, and it had given me (and the others, I'm sure) a long pause for thought. I still took a lot of risks in painting, but the outcome if I failed was only that I looked foolish, not dead. And I always learned something, whether the risk worked or not. This was the second time Maya had been kidnapped, and the first time it happened I'd been forced to kill a federal officer to free her. As I sat near the fountain listening to Cody hooting in the background I couldn't help wondering whether the next time one or more of us was not going to walk away. If it happened this time, it would be my doing, and for no more than the $500 retainer from Clarissa Phelps. The phrase *skewed priorities* crossed my mind. I didn't like to think of myself as chasing a principle, but I couldn't see what else to call it.

Finally I went back in to say goodbye to Maya and got the number of Glass's cell phone, which Cody had forgotten to do, since she'd called on our landline.

When we settled back out by the fountain he looked pointedly at my cigar.

"You know, I think I'd like one of those too, now. It's not good for my blood pressure, but what the hell. Maya can sure be scrappy when the situation calls for it."

"And other times too. She killed Perry Watt, as you recall."

"And Mercy Buchanan." This was a woman who had ambushed us on our last case.

"That's right." I went in and got him a Monte Cristo and a cognac.

"Glass won't call the cops once he gets loose," Cody said, after he lit it. "He's got to get her back, and she could just produce the paintings to support her side of the story. Do you feel like killing him?"

"Of course. But I'm not going to unless I have to. I'd rather get the art back and notify the museums that lost it. He'll be on the run and he'll lose everything except the money he's got spirited away. That'll be more fun."

"He'll be expecting us, or you anyway."

"Like you said at the Bellas Artes; never assume you know how many of them are coming at you."

"He might still know how many of us there are

from the guys who stopped us." He blew a long plume of smoke at Orlando, our resident garden grackle, who was watching him with hopeful interest from beneath the leaves of a bromeliad.

"Even so. I think we're up to it this time. We've got Maya, the head of the agency, and she's mad. Remember how she castrated Otto Koerner with a machete in Oaxaca?"

"Don't mess with Maya," he said. "I'm not always sure what she's capable of, but I know it's true."

Of course, we had no guns anymore ourselves, and it was too complicated to buy new ones here and try to cross the border into the States with them, so we decided to buy them in Baker Falls, and then get rid of them before we came back, since bringing them into México was illegal, although the drug cartels got them from their American customers by the semi-load. After all, it was Texas, and we could expense them to the museums when they paid us for our recovery efforts. Some of these cases can be more speculative than others. I felt like calling Clarissa Phelps and hooting, but decided to wait until we'd gotten Maya and the old masters back into México.

That afternoon we caught a shuttle van to the Leon airport and boarded a flight into Baker Falls that would arrive about 5:30. I had Maya's passport with me. We had at first thought we could rent another van in

Baker Falls and bring the paintings with us, and return the van later and fly back. But when I went online to check on the legalities of this, it appeared that we couldn't cross the border driving anything but a vehicle registered to one of us. Even if we bought one in Baker Falls it would still probably take weeks to get the title from the Texas motor vehicle department. None of us had that kind of time. If we were going to shoot it out with Glass and his friends I wanted to do it on our own turf, where Delgado was used to such things and would take a more tolerant attitude if we killed one or all of them. A lot of things in México are about being connected, and his was one connection that had already paid off royally. With all the people we'd killed collectively, none of us had ever been arrested.

"Here's what we can do," said Cody as we rose over the broccoli fields after takeoff. "We rent a van and drive down to Laredo with the paintings, arranging to turn it in there. Once in place, we find a guy with another van—his own—who can take us across the border. In the first town on the México side, we buy a vehicle for ourselves and we're home free. Then we sell it to one of the dealers at a loss when we get back here. Certain hard costs are always associated with these deals."

"Sounds good to me." I liked the geometry of loading $40 million worth of stolen old masters into some dirt farmer's van. What better cover could there be? Suddenly I felt like Bernhard Glass.

"Did you bring enough money?"

"No, but I can wire it to the dealer from any Internet cafe," I said. "No problem."

Although Baker Falls was probably a twelve-hour drive from San Miguel, by plane it was only two hours, mostly through cloudless skies above a landscape that increasingly flattened out into brown cattle country, etched by meandering arroyos. Half an hour into the flight the cabin attendant came by with declaration forms. We had nothing to list but evil intentions, and they were hard to put a value on. Coming in over Baker Falls, we could see the modest downtown, with a handful of ten or twelve story buildings and a single freeway snaking through it.

I had called the car rental from home before we left, and on arrival we were given the same kind of Ford van that the loading crew at the Bellas Artes had used. They had no problem about dropping it off in Laredo. My cell wasn't getting a signal, so I called Maya from a pay phone in the airport. Two blocks from the warehouse where she'd stashed the paintings, she was holed up in a $42 motel. She was eager to wrap it up and leave Baker Falls, nervous that the VRC director had figured out where they were and already recovered them. She hadn't dared to go back to check on them alone, fearing she'd run into half a dozen armed art-lovers. I caught the freeway outside the airport perimeter and exited ten minutes later at State Street.

The Sojourner Motel was state-of-the-art seventies design, two stories high with all the rooms overlooking the parking lot. We climbed the outside stairs and stopped at room 226. Cody did his policeman's knock.

"Who is it?" Maya's voice was eager, yet edgy.

"Peoria Police, open up. We know you're in there."

The door swung open and hit the wall inside. Maya rushed into my arms. I kissed her for a long time, and then she kissed Cody all over his face and neck. She had a Glock nine millimeter in the waistband of a pair of green slacks I'd never seen before. They weren't up to her standard. For one thing, they were too loose in the waistband and too short in the ankles.

"Nice room," I said, walking in. A tangerine bedspread, dark green plastic headboard molded to look like green wood, whatever tree that would be. Over the bed hung a photo of the Baker Falls skyline at night. It was more impressive than what we'd seen after we landed. The carpet was mottled brown shag with one path worn from the bed to the entry and another to the bathroom.

She tossed the room key on the bedside table and we left. Although I could see the profile of a switchblade through the fabric of her left back pocket, she was traveling light.

Three minutes later I pulled up in the loading zone in front of an orange brick warehouse. A few other cars were parked on the street, but none were occupied, and no one moved about on foot. The area had the feeling of a business district after hours. Maya unlocked a steel door and we went in.

"We forgot the guns," said Cody as he punched the button at the freight elevator. "I'm off my game." Maya pulled out the Glock and gave it to him handle first. On the third floor he stuck his head over the slatted gate and looked around, in both directions. Then I lifted the gate.

"It's down toward the end on the right, nearly at the window," Maya said.

We chose a cart from several along the wall and moved down the corridor. Cody put his finger to his lips, although anyone could have heard the cart clattering over the plank floor. Maya stopped before the second door from the end. The one next to it also had a lock, but three others on the same wall didn't. "I'm going to cover you," Cody whispered to me. "Pull the pictures out and stack them on the cart as I watch. I don't like this at all." He moved toward one of the empty facing cubicles at the opposite end and went inside, closing the door partially. Maya and I looked at each other, taking a long breath before she inserted the key in the padlock. She always complained a lot about risk, but when it came down to the nubbin, like now, she was always up to it. *Always.*

I heard a subtle click as the lock on our door came open. Maya yanked the padlock free and swung it open. At the same instant I saw the door next to us start to move slowly, just a crack, then faster. Two shots rang out, echoing down the corridor as Maya and I leaped inside the cubicle. I turned and saw a man fall across our doorway. He was lying still on his back, with two crimson patches spreading on his chest just an inch apart. They merged and spread outward. This was the man we had tied up and gagged in San Miguel. Cody bent over his body and felt his neck, then, shaking his head, dragged him back into the neighboring cubicle where he'd been hiding.

"He's gone," he said, coming out. He shut the door without a sound. Cody placed Maya's padlock on the door and snapped it shut. "They'll find him when he starts to smell. We'll be across the border by then. Nice gun, by the way. But I still think I like a revolver better. They never jam. You can get a misfire from a bad round, but then you just pull the trigger again. I left this guy's gun with him. You never know what else he might have done with it. The cops might want to look into it when they find his body." His voice was cooler than his face.

"Aren't you upset?" asked Maya, as she loaded one of the boxed pictures onto the cart. She would have been shrieking if we hadn't been getting ready to get out of there with a multi-million dollar cargo.

"Of course I'm upset. The man was going to kill you. I saw his face. Now let's get this stuff out of here."

"So Glass knew we were coming back," I said, lifting four million dollars worth of art onto the cart with one hand.

"I'm not sure he knew it, but he must have suspected that Maya hadn't gotten the pictures out. Hopefully, he didn't know exactly where they were. If he'd known it, his people would have all been here waiting for us, and the art would have been long gone."

"And so would we," said Maya. "End of story."

She stopped short of saying it was now over, and eight minutes later we walked out of the warehouse and loaded the cases into our rental van. Cody's well-honed cop instincts hadn't faded in seven years of retirement, so it was no surprise when, after we'd driven a couple of blocks, he said, "I can see a newer Mercedes in the line behind us about four cars back. I can't be sure, but I think they've made us. It's probably Glass himself with that car."

The warehouse where he had stored the pictures was one of eight lined up in two parallel rows that faced a pair of railroad tracks running between them. Cody swung around the corner, looked down the tracks and gave a small whoop. "We've got them now, if I can pull this off." As we crossed the tracks I saw a long freight headed our way in a normal in-town manner. In the other direction, the tracks curved away from the high-rise area. The train was about a block down, and Cody swung left toward it on the street beyond, accelerating. I turned to see the Mercedes speed up and pull away from the cluster of cars that had given it cover.

We flashed down the street and, without warning, cut out of the line of traffic and spun around back toward the tracks in the direction we'd come, flying over them with just fifteen or twenty feet to spare as the engineer blew his whistle at us. The last I saw of the Mercedes was as it pulled up and stopped as the train crossed the street, blocking its path. We turned right at the corner and drove down toward the tail of the train and waited for it to pass two blocks away. When the caboose cleared the intersection, we headed south out of town, the way we'd originally been going.

"You've done this before," I said.

"Seen it done. Maybe Bruce Willis did it, but I'm not sure. In the past I was usually the one waiting behind the train as the other car disappeared. They'll never know we doubled back. That guy Glass may know his art, but he doesn't know pursuit. That's what this is about now, and it will be going forward. The balance shifts."

An hour and a half later we were in a poor Hispanic neighborhood in Laredo, looking for an old van. It offered many to choose from. Cody pulled up behind a 15-year-old Dodge in front of a shotgun house with two young men sitting on the porch.

"*Buenos dias*," I said, approaching the porch. They were surprised when I addressed them in Spanish. "I need a ride across the border for three of us and seven flat boxes. I'll pay $250 if you can drop us in Nuevo Laredo after we turn in this rental van. We can't take it into México." The two looked at each other as if it was the strangest thing they'd ever heard, but still of considerable interest.

"And you will pay for the gas, too, *señor*?" asked one after a moment. I think he sensed I wasn't ready to negotiate.

"Of course. I'll fill the tank. But I have a question. You are legal and you have a passport, right? You'll need to get back across."

"I was born here. *No hay problema*."

I gave him two $50 bills. "I'll give you the rest when you drop us off on the other side of the border."

Thirty minutes later we were in line at customs with a full tank, and our rental Ford already back at the car rental. Maya was in the passenger seat like she was this guy's wife. That would never have happened—his skin was about fourteen shades darker than hers. Cody and I were sitting on the floor next to the pictures to keep them from flying around. A border guard on the Méxican side paused at the driver's door and handed our driver a declaration form. "I will also need your passports, please." We passed them up, with our visas.

Cody started filling out the customs declaration. "What's the value of this stuff?"

"Forty million or more, but I wouldn't put that down. Just put $1400. That's $200 per package." The driver passed the form back to the inspector, then reached out the window and punched a button, and a red light lit up. It meant stop for inspection. The border cop pointed at a line of cars to one side.

"Please pull out and wait over there."

"You're sure there's no duty on art?" asked Maya,

once we were moving.

"None, going in or out. I've shipped things up here before, even to Canada."

Forty-five minutes later we were at the head of the line and two officials pulled out the boxes.

"This is it," I said to Cody. "Try to look innocent." The border people opened the boxes at the side of the van. I couldn't see them anymore, but they were making noises of bewilderment. Maybe they'd never seen seventeenth century old masters before. One man returned to the back doors.

"You have said this is art on your form?"

"Yes." Where was this going? He walked back around the side.

In a moment he returned and tore off a sheet of paper from a pad he was carrying. I looked at it.

"Fifty-six pesos import duty?" That was a bit more than four dollars.

"Yes. Under the category of forest products." He must have meant the two landscapes.

"You are certain of this?"

"*Señor*, what you have are fourteen pieces of plywood in those boxes. Nothing else besides the padding. I don't know much about art, but I see no images on them. Perhaps you can explain?"

I knew of only one explanation; we were idiots. "My mistake," I said lamely. "I thought we had brought something else." I reached in my pocket for my wallet and gave them seventy pesos. "Keep the change." Here you can tip even the customs people.

"I guess the folks in the Mercedes weren't after the boxes," Maya said grimly as we drove away. "They only wanted to kill us. That's comforting to know." Her lips were set in a straight line no more than a millimeter wide.

We had the van driver drop us at the bus station instead of at a car dealer. I paid him off and started to unload the boxes at a trashcan outside, but he stopped me.

"I wonder if I could have those, *señor*, since you are going to throw them away?" He shrugged. I shrugged too. Everything has value here, to someone.

We took the first class ETN bus from Nuevo Laredo back to San Miguel. No one had much to say on the way. Eight hours of dry, sunbaked scenery didn't inspire any wisdom; it was an area the early Spanish settlers had largely ignored, as having no agricultural potential except beef cattle. At that point ranching was still way down their list. It would start to gain in importance once they'd stripped the silver from the mountains. The presence of major copper deposits was only revealed much later.

It was obvious the paintings hadn't remained long in that warehouse after Maya left, and it was equally clear that we were going to have to try a little harder to beat Glass at this game. No Paul Zacher Reference Collection would ever be formed. This particular round went to our driver, with $250 of my money, nearly a full tank of gas, and fourteen rectangles of plywood, customs duty paid.

As we got into a cab at the San Miguel bus station many hours later, Maya slammed the door. The driver turned to look at her in surprise.

"*Todo por nada*," she hissed at him. "And I was even kidnapped, *otra vez*, again!" The driver's hands both went up in bewilderment.

"Don't blame yourself," said Cody. "You did

great, capturing Glass like that. I was impressed that you didn't kill him. Restraint can be a big part of this, especially in a heated moment, which you've had your fair share of. We just didn't have time to check those boxes, that was the problem."

"And you have the rest of his money," I said. "Even though we had to throw his gun out the window on the way to the border."

"Two hundred and seventy-five dollars remained of it. Piffle! Three nights at Harry's for an agency celebration. No reason to celebrate now."

"And, it more than paid for the van rental," said Cody, ignoring this. "Something just occurred to me, though. What if the cops find the gun back there and compare it with the bullets they found in the guy at the warehouse? Then they trace it to Glass, who I'm sure must have registered it, being such an upstanding citizen. He's going to have considerable explaining to do, since he probably didn't report it stolen. Especially since the victim can most likely be shown to have been in Glass's employ, killed in a warehouse where Glass rented space."

"Then we should have left it in a more obvious place," said Maya.

It looked to me like we were clutching at anything that sounded remotely optimistic. "I wish Sheila Roper had seen this coming," I said. Next she'd be calling to tell me Maya was back in México.

"So you were painting someone else while I was gone?"

"I was painting nothing, only worrying about you." I went on to tell her about our psychic visitor.

"It was the cleaners that she saw. It had a room

for the steam machine. But what happens next?"

"We start by buying ourselves a couple of .38s from that shady guy at the Tuesday Market," said Cody. "And right away. They'll be coming after us soon. They can look us up in *Juarde*, like Sheila Roper did."

CHAPTER 9
DR. BERNHARD GLASS

Dr. Bernhard Glass, Ph.D., [as Aaron Herschel Levi, University of Illinois, 1980] had things other than connoisseurship on his mind at the moment. It was not that he didn't take the Paul Zacher Agency seriously—he had never before had a knife at his throat, and would not soon forget the sensation. Although she was hot in her own dark way, he felt that Méxican broad was too wild for his taste. What he now had on his plate was the most outrageous theft he'd ever contemplated. And since it would be taking place inside México, he didn't need any more publicity from the San Miguel fiasco at the moment, or ever. He was now especially grateful that Collin Welch had not found it necessary to kill Zacher, although he clearly deserved it. That event could be penciled onto the schedule for later, reserved for a less hectic time. For the moment, the painter could sit in San Miguel and contemplate his fourteen pieces of half-inch construction-grade plywood. He had no way of knowing what was coming next. Glass was almost rubbing his chubby hands thinking about it.

The director's new Glock Nine rested in his desk drawer, freshly loaded. His inner office door had been newly fitted with a remote control lock that could be released by a buzzer below his desktop, and a security camera now scanned the outer office in broad sweeps. The genuine Pissarro hanging behind him during Zacher's visit had been removed and stored with the other stolen pictures, replaced by a phony Vermeer from Han van Meegeren's early period. This had come to the VRC from one of Andrew Mellon's heirs who had already paid the estate tax on it some years before. Glass didn't spend much time looking at it; it was not van Meegeren's best work, and lacked the unique presence that genuine Vermeers always had. It did have a strong provenance, having been passed on as genuine by Bernard Berenson himself in the thirties, before the era of UV lamps. From his own research, Glass knew it had been painted in 1928.

His secretary put through a call and Glass found Natty Bollander on the other end.

"I'm here in México," Bollander said. "I've got all the equipment."

"Perfect. You will find waiting for you at general delivery in the main post office a tube of three different prints of our objective. They are addressed to you at Glassworks, general delivery. As I said before, they are not from Skirra, but from what I could find, they're the best available. If they differ at all, use your best judgment. I haven't looked at them myself, except on the Internet, so the resolution wasn't the best."

"This is making me just a bit nervous; I don't like to make artistic decisions. What are the canvas requirements?"

"I've already taken care of it. At the hotel desk you'll find waiting for you an old piece of linen of inferior quality about twenty-eight by fifty-four inches. How old doesn't really matter, they would never allow a piece to be clipped from the original for carbon dating. You need only an appearance that isn't new-looking. You will be using no stretchers, so clamp it to a board as you work. Don't use nails because I don't want any punctures in it. The literature will suggest that it's really made from miraculously-surviving maguey fiber, but that can't be true. It would have disintegrated centuries ago. It can only be linen to have held up this long."

"This sounds like the Shroud of Turin, only smaller."

"Not quite. You will be recreating the *tilma* of Juan Diego, the national religious icon of México."

"Jesus Christ!"

"No. In this case it is the Virgin Mary, Our Lady of Guadalupe. Now you see why Skirra was no help on this one."

Natty covered the receiver and looked for Chiara, but she was in the bathroom. "And you're going to steal the original?"

"That's what I do, Natty. Just suck it up. An Illinois phrase, by the way."

"And this is going to a collector?"

"A quite wealthy one who believes the icon is more appropriately held by a devout individual in his own private chapel, rather than open to the view of a vulgar public. I believe he's even a member of Opus Dei."

"And how will you get it out of the country? Once it comes out that it's stolen, the borders will be sealed tighter than a drum."

"For one thing, I won't have to, the buyer lives in México. For another, if you do your job right, no one will know it's gone after we make the switch. When it comes off tour, the image will be remounted fifteen feet above the congregation as it is now, and no one is allowed to approach it closely. The worshipful visitors pass it on a moving walkway, like at the airport. They don't even have the option to pause and kneel. It is only examined for condition once in two generations, so it isn't likely that the scientist who sees it next has ever seen it before. That examination for this round will only be cursory, scanning for condition issues, according to my sources. It will have been done just before we make the switch. That's the nice feature of this; no museum professionals will be poking at it. We have only the gullible adherents to deal with. As we know, the need to believe trumps everything else. That's your advantage."

"I see." But what Natty also saw was that now he was going to attempt to copy a painting that, according to tradition, had never been painted at all. It was thought by the devout to be a miraculous application of the Virgin's image to the front of the sixteenth century Indian's mantle, a *tilma*, using no earthly materials or techniques. Natty prided himself on being able to reproduce nearly anything painted, but this was going to be a stretch. Although not a believer, he had never before been called upon to compete with an act of God.

After he finished with Dr. Glass, Natty plugged his laptop into the Internet connection in his hotel room and fired it up. He didn't trust wi-fi for something like this. Chiara emerged from the bathroom and turned on the television. He Googled the search topic in English, thereby avoiding the three million mentions in Spanish, but hundreds of thousands still confronted him.

The story was simple. In the desert near México City, a poor Indian named Juan Diego saw a vision of a young woman on December 9, 1531. She instructed him to build a church on that spot. It is not recorded whether he thought this request odd. He went to the bishop, who asked for some proof. Juan Diego returned to the place of the vision and saw the lady again. She instructed him to fill his poncho with roses, which were growing out of season, and give them to the bishop. When he appeared in the bishop's palace he opened his poncho to show him the roses, but instead the cloth (*the tilma*) showed a picture of the lady he had seen. Now known as Our Lady of Guadalupe, she is the patron saint of México. The *tilma*, displayed in its own cathedral, is the greatest pilgrimage destination in the Americas.

Opinions varied as to what the image really was, aside from being the likeness of the mother of Christ. Natty was surprised to discover that a number of scientific examinations had been conducted over the years, with differing explanations that depended on the level of faith of the investigator. One flatly stated it to be the only heavenly relic in existence on earth, produced on maguey fibers that had miraculously outlasted their normal twenty to thirty-year lifespan. No conventional pigments or brushwork had been detected. With a frown, Chiara took a chair next to him at this point and read over his shoulder.

Another report said that the fabric was not maguey at all, but common hand-made linen of an early period. This was a material that lasted well if protected from the elements, but not a fabric an impoverished Méxican Indian would be wearing in the 1530s. Furthermore, the current surface of the object had been painted with conventional brushes, and the top layer was merely the most recent in a series of three. If the image was nearly 500 years old, and had been on public display for most of that period, two restorations made sense to Natty.

Lab analysis of the pigments suggested earth and animal origins; soot, carmine from cochineal—an early export in colonial days—and mineral blues possibly from turquoise or naturally occurring copper sulfate. Natty began to relax a bit. This was looking more like his home turf.

But a third report stopped him cold.

Reflected in the pupils of the lady's eyes, he read, were the images of the thirteen witnesses present at the time the icon was unveiled to the bishop, immediately after it appeared. Their forms were even curved to follow the contour of the eye itself. Keeping pace with him in the text, Chiara said, "What kind of brush would do that?" Natty groaned. It wouldn't be one he'd ever seen.

Thirteen people painted in less than an eighth of an inch—more like a sixteenth, since the figure was just over half of life size. He almost reached for the phone to call Dr. Glass back and tell him it couldn't be done. But if the image were mounted high off the floor, and not closely examined for another twenty years or more, who would know the pupils were blank? By that time the theft of the Juan Diego *tilma* would be ancient history. Natty himself would be retired to a small peach-colored villa on the Adriatic, at last free to work out the parameters of his own elusive creative vision. That day would be his reward for all the things like this he'd come up against in the service of Dr. Glass's endeavors.

Perhaps the Church would even hush it up, if

they ever found out about the switch, since, as the premier pilgrimage draw in the Americas, it was a great moneymaker, second only to St. Peter's in Rome as a pilgrimage site worldwide. Who would come to see it, if it were revealed that it had been replaced by a copy? He realized he could absolutely count on the Church to back him up. As an unbeliever, this was a sensation he'd never had before. Maybe that last part about the eyes was pious baloney anyway. From the perspective of a non-practicing Church of England dropout, México was full of that, he thought, as was Florence, with all the little saintly corpses behind glass beneath the altars. Surely they were extensively maintained, decade by decade, with all the tricks of the mortician's trade. More than this, he didn't want to know, even though those people were, in a sense, forgers much like he was, halting the effects of death.

A few minutes later, modestly hopeful, but at the same time full of misgiving, Natty and Chiara left for the post office, watching the crowded streets as they walked. They had left their wallets and purses locked up in the hotel room. Even in Italy, they had heard that México City could be a tough place. It required the same vigilance as walking down any street in Naples or Palermo.

Back at the hotel Natty unrolled the three prints of the Virgin of Guadalupe from their tubes, relieved to see they were identical but for the quality of reproduction. He selected the best one for detail and tossed the others in the wastebasket, then sat and stared at it. Even under the magnifying glass he'd brought with him, he found nothing in the Virgin's pupils but a dark dot. Don't sweat the small stuff, he said to himself. Although he always worked in isolation, Natty began to see himself as part of a larger group in this case, one that fostered and maintained illusions on a national scale.

He had also learned from the Internet that, although plausible references to the image and its origin appeared as early as the 1540s, the poor Indian's *tilma* had never been publicly shown until more than 100 years later. This was in itself a strong suggestion that the picture had been painted to confirm the legend. But since it had proved such a powerful inducement for Indian conversion, if it had been genuine, why hadn't it been shown immediately? The Church had never been slow to recognize such opportunities. Obviously it had taken Church authorities a while to come up with a suitable image. On the basis of this alone, it looked like the fulfillment of an old rumor, rather than the origin of one.

From his broad experience as a copyist, Natty had also immediately noticed it did not look like other sixteenth century devotional pictures, examples of which were to be seen everywhere in Florence. Before hooking up with Dr. Glass, he had painted dozens of them. When the Renaissance arrived throughout Europe in the late 1400s, new styles of painting had emerged, but at first only for secular subjects, which themselves were new. No conventions had yet been established about how to depict ermine robes and crystal goblets, velvet cloaks next to steaming tables of lobster and oysters, bowls of grapes and pomegranates. The emerging style was much more open to innovation as it catered to a new middle class, who were themselves unaccustomed to owning paintings Certainly none had been left to them by their parents or grandparents.

Although Michelangelo and Raphael were

pioneering new methods to portray religious subjects, paintings commissioned by the Church from average painters continued to display older, more conservative images. There was no reason to change, since the underlying beliefs hadn't. Understandably, adoption of the newer ideas for most church work lagged by at least 100 years, except from the most advanced Renaissance artists, and this painting Natty had to copy was not the work of one of those. The elements he saw in this print were nearly all later, easily seventeenth century. The great relic he was to copy had to be a pious hoax, if only on the basis of the design elements that made up the image.

Paintings are assembled from visual components the way a building is made from bricks and mortar, things that can be dated. The ones Natty was looking at were not the elements of the period when Don Diego was said to have appeared before the archbishop wearing this *tilma.*

Natty was relieved. His task had become the forging of an ancient forgery, not much different from forging any genuine, but earthly work. The story of the thirteen human images within the pupils had to be a hoax he could ignore, unverifiable at fifteen feet off the floor, or even at an inch away. Examining the print closely, he was beginning to doubt whether the picture had even been painted in México. More probably it had been done in Spain, where the legend of Our Lady of Guadalupe originated. He scanned the image in detail for a signature, but saw none. Church pictures usually didn't have them. Most painters then were merely craftsmen.

He could see now how it must have happened. Some cleric had come across the image in a Spanish church, and had the sudden inspiration to bring it to México and pass it off as the Juan Diego *tilma*—the inspirational story had already made the rounds. The linen canvas had been trimmed to the *tilma* shape, eliminating the folds and nail marks from stretching it over the original wooden bars. It might once have been part of a significantly larger painting.

Natty sat back in his chair. He knew seventeenth century pigments; they were the same throughout Europe but for the cochineal, and that would already have been imported into Spain from its new colonies in the Americas, but not much further because Spain restricted this trade to its own territories. Looking at the colors in the print, which he hoped were at least close to the original, he began making a list of what he would need. Before he went to the art supply store he could go to the cathedral and check the original against his visual memory of the print to verify the accuracy of the colors.

Some time later Chiara moved up behind him and put her hands on his shoulders. Still a marginal Catholic, she knew what the image was.

"You have solved it, right? I know that look."

"I think so."

"But what will you do with it when its finished?"

"Send it off to my customer, of course."

"Isn't it strange that all these customers always want copies painted by hand, when they could have the good reproductions, like this one? Wouldn't that be much cheaper? The quality of this one is not bad, is it?"

When he didn't respond she suddenly had an unwelcome insight and pulled her hands away as if she'd touched something unpleasant. Her beloved artist was only a copyist. She'd always assumed his work included original paintings too, but now she saw it probably didn't. He would never produce anything fresh and original. This explained why he never hung any of his own pictures on the walls of his studio, only reproductions in the process of drying until they were shipped out. Natty had never shown in a gallery. Never, since she met him, had he even searched for one to represent his work.

Some time later when he asked Chiara to accompany him to the cathedral where the relic was on view for its last day before going on tour, she pled a headache. When he left, she searched his laptop for his financial records. Aside from regular but unremarkable remittances from the Pitti and Uffizi galleries in Florence, she found a series of substantial deposits from a company called Glassworks Pty., Ltd., London. Was Natty designing stained glass windows too, now? Was he inching his way into his own creativity through a lesser medium, one less threatening?

Chiara moved away from the desk and sat down on the comfortable chair by the bed, feeling she had lost something that she'd never questioned before. While it was true that Natty was showing no sign of asking her to marry him, as long as she'd imagined him being a successful painter one day, she'd been better able to rationalize staying with him. Now, being the thirty-something girlfriend of an art forger who showed no prospects of breaking through into the legitimate painting world seemed like both an unacceptable drop in status and a major boost in risk. And what was happening with these copies?

If her life was ever going to change, she'd have to change it herself. She felt a subtle shift in the balance of power between them.

CHAPTER 10

Thinking back over the people the Zacher Agency had come up against, I had to admit that, while their employees were rarely the best, the leadership was often formidable, both in intelligence and in finely developed criminal instincts. Our encounter with Antonio Trujillo on our last case was a good example; we had to come up against him twice before he was taken out. It looked like Glass was not going to let the team down in this respect. I wondered if he might be smarter than I am.

I wasn't thinking this because he had a Ph.D. I'd known more than a few doctoral candidates when I was in school, and for most of them, the P was likely to stand for Persistent more often than Profound, and in some cases, Plodding. Many of them felt official certification was a plausible substitute for insight or talent, and it was certainly easier to come by. Experience has given me sufficient respect for my own intelligence. I don't feel inferior to anyone in that respect, but my intelligence is more of a diagonal variety than you usually come across. It doesn't come out of my forehead like a beacon on a miner's helmet, illuminating all before it. A lot of what I know about painting is in my eye and my hand, and in the right side of my brain, so it can't be put into words. I don't disparage it for that reason. But at the end of the day, although Maya had neatly gotten away from him, Glass had still beaten us on the paintings, and that was what this case was about. I felt we weren't doing that well this time around.

"How can we get that bastard down here on our own turf?" I said to her. She was tucked in next to me on the sofa. "I don't think we can kidnap him like they did you."

"No. But what's his weakness? Maybe it's too long since you were in school to remember. A man like that has to have weaknesses, not that all of them don't, and probably more than one. Just the look of him says he's self-indulgent. His neck wobbles like a turkey when he talks."

"I think I can recall a few strawberry blond MFA candidates who brought him to his knees. At least that was the story that went around."

"So he was someone who appreciated the student body. But you always seem to think it's going to be about women. Sometimes you miss the other distractions in life."

"I'll give you that. He must have had other distractions too."

"What painters did he like?"

"As I recall, his tastes were wide-ranging, right up through Abstract Expressionism. Naturally, he knows his subject. You can't fault him there."

"Anyone special?"

I hadn't thought much about Bernhard Glass over the years. I have a tendency to forget about people or things in my past that were problematical. Until the VRC show, his name had never reentered my consciousness, and it took me a while to pull up his tastes.

"Matisse," I said, after a few minutes while my

brain spun in neutral. "He loves Matisse. Not the paper cutouts of dancers and the chapel glass designs of his later years when he was bedridden, but the paintings of his late middle period, in the twenties and early thirties. I agree with Glass on that, although I never cared for Picasso, who Matisse is always associated with. Matisse had a color sense Picasso never reached, and a more fluid design to his work. He also lacked Picasso's taste for violence. I don't think Matisse was ever as angry. Anger gets in the way of art; it's too often political. And you know what I think of politics."

"I wonder if Glass would like to steal a Matisse," she said, in a tone she reserved for surveying human weaknesses, mostly men's, "or own one that's been stolen. I didn't see any on the museum lists I worked up. What if we could tempt him with one? Maybe no one is faking Matisse now, like they are Picasso. You would know."

I thought about this for a while. Then something came to me.

"How about tempting him with fourteen?"

"We gave away the plywood back at the border, if that's what you're thinking. But I don't see how that connects."

"No, it doesn't. But if they're all still together, then someone out there has fourteen Matisses," I said, "and nobody knows who. The number is just a coincidence. During the War, Matisse stayed on in France, but he lived in the south, on the Riviera, where the Germans didn't occupy the country. Instead they had the Vichy government as a puppet of the Nazis. Anyway, when Hermann Goering got on his degenerate art crusade, the prefect of Nice, where Matisse was living, used it as an excuse to raid his studio and confiscate fourteen paintings he said were degenerate. They were never recovered after the War. Now they're worth many millions, of course. The artist was never able to get them back. He won in court, in 1946, but afterward he couldn't find them. I've always thought they might have gone to Germany, or if they were in East Germany before reunification, then they might have gone to Russia."

"In that case you can kiss them goodbye. But what if we could dangle them in front of Glass's nose anyway?"

"If we had them," I said. "You don't ask much. But no records of them exist. They weren't ever photographed, and no one knows what they looked like."

"Seems like that gives you a free hand, doesn't it?" Maya gave me her sweetest look. "We probably wouldn't need more than two to convince Glass that we had them all, right?"

Maya did know how to get me going. Surely I could do two Matisses in his style of the early thirties. It wouldn't hurt that I was already a fan of this period of his work. The pigments would be the same ones I use now, although I don't think he used titanium white. It would have been only lead white for him. And lead primer on linen for a base. We could doctor the linen with coffee and a little bleach here and there, and add some scuffmarks. Blow some finely pulverized dirt over the back, the kind that rises from the cobblestone streets here in clouds in the dry season. The paintings had to appear to be only about seventy-five years old. Coat the stretchers with mud for a while and then soak them in watery tea for a day. I knew a cabinetmaker here in San Miguel who kept a supply of wormy pine on hand for antique drawer fronts. I could have him run me some stretchers. He'd think it was a waste of wood with good character, but he'd still do it. Anything custom made here costs about the same as off-the-shelf.

They wouldn't have to fool Sotheby's or the Metropolitan Museum, only a self-important connoisseur named Glass, who'd only be looking at them online. He'd be thrown back on his own esthetic judgment, since no photo images could be found to compare them to. This would be fun; the kind of problem I enjoy. I went up to the studio bookshelves and pulled out my Matisse book and blew the dust off the top edge of the pages.

The elements were all in place within those illustrations; but I wouldn't copy any particular picture, because it was already published. Matisse favored using the same props and characters again and again, in different groupings. The task was to plausibly recombine once more what he'd already used several times in different contexts. I suddenly saw it as a challenge: was Paul Zacher, the artist, smarter than Dr. Glass, the academic connoisseur? Was being a real painter better than having a Ph.D. in art history? We were about to find out, and I was primed and ready.

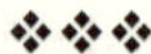

Maya phoned Cody. She always had more leverage with him than I did. If bullets were flying toward each of us, he'd stop the one coming at her first with his own body, then, bleeding, he would check to see how badly I'd been hit. I didn't expect to hear all of their conversation, only her side of it. But when she pulled up a chair and sat next to me in the studio, Cody's voice was big enough to catch that close.

"What if I had a stack of fourteen Matisse paintings," she said, "none of them ever seen before, that I wanted to fence. Suppose I had a target client in the States. What would I do?"

"In that case, I'd put my lovely face on the front of the deal and he couldn't resist it."

Hearing this gave me some insight into what their conversations were like when I wasn't around. She always encouraged him, and he lapped it up.

"Paul's sitting right next to me," she said, with a glance my way, "and the target is Bernhard Glass. Obviously, my face would only put him off, after our last meeting." A minor pause followed while Cody regrouped.

"You're trying to get him down here. I can see that. You want Delgado to bust him for the murder of Ortíz, the burglar."

"Yes," she said, "and the minor issue of kidnapping me. But I don't think we can say the paintings are in San Miguel in the beginning. It'll only tip him off."

"Why say any location at all? Let's bait the hook first. What's the lure?"

"Paul's going to paint two Matisses of his middle period."

"OK. I'll talk to Chicago and find out who's fencing high end art in the U.S., and you get me photos of the new Matisses as soon as he's finished with them."

I thought it was a strong tribute to me that he didn't for a moment question my ability to paint them, but it didn't make me think he knew what they were like, either.

"Here's the visual vocabulary," I said, after she hung up. "Both would be room settings, with vines and other large-leaf foliage, standing screens on the floor, and grill work on the windows. Dark-haired women in harem pants or no pants at all, brocade upholstery, patterned wallpaper. Lush colors and curvy lines. It's a piece of cake."

"And you won't need a model? Or should I pose?"

"The detail is vague or nonexistent, and his overall brushwork is coarse, but controlled. I'll just make it up. His models were always fleshier than you are anyway. He liked to show little bellies and wide hips on his women—you're not constructed that way."

"How about his brushstroke? Do you remember it?"

"Not exactly, but I can fake it. If Glass gets close enough to bend over and study it, I'll drop a net on him. Game over."

"How long do you think it will it take? Two weeks?"

"Five or six days, tops."

The physical painting of each one could probably be done in a single day, but I planned to allow myself enough time to properly plan the concepts while I was having the stretchers made. What I didn't mention to her was that I was sick of the antique religious subjects I'd been working on for my collector in Guadalajara, and this would be a welcome break. Matisse possessed a sensuous joy that most of the old saints had missed. Maybe they'd been expecting to connect with it after death. Good luck on that.

"What if it doesn't work?" she said. Maya was never an easy sell, even when it was her own idea.

"Then we'll have two pretty decent Matisses that the world has never seen before."

"We could give one to Cody, since we don't have a client paying us on this case."

"Sure. I'll put a linebacker in one of them, with wide hips and a small charming tummy."

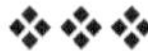

Of course I knew that this was what connected me to the Vergruen Reference Collection or to any skillful fakes at all: I was a happy forger at heart. It fascinated me. I would have loved to see my own work hanging in the VRC's group show at the Bellas Artes, but that idea had one serious problem—I insisted on signing my own name on the back of anything I copied. It was like saying, hey, I could have been this guy too, so look at what I'm really doing under my own name! Not that I was going to do that with the Matisses—at least, not right away. I'd wait until we'd snookered Glass and locked him up. In his densely sober way, he would have said that I lacked proper seriousness as a forger. *Gravitas* might be the word he'd use. The word I'd use was *fun.*

Perhaps he'd be right, because I never faked my own work; each piece was as real as I could make it. Later I was ruminating in the studio about the first of the Matisse fakes when my cell rang. It was Cody.

"We have a deal, I think," he said, "once you're ready with the two paintings. Chicago liked the idea and connected me with this guy named Gerson. I think they'll watch from behind the scenes, as much as they can, the way he sets this up. That's not his real name, of course, and he and the police pretend to each other that he's retired and only counsels them on art theft now and then when it comes up on a case. In return, they leave him alone if he doesn't get too far out of line. It's going to cost some money, but we can expense it to the case."

"We don't have a client."

"Then expense it to yourself like you did the air tickets to Texas and Minneapolis. You've still got that big wad of money from the Malcolm Brendel case, I assume, and I get the impression this business has a personal component for you."

"True," I said. "Twenty years I've been a painter and I'm still a sucker for fakes."

"Maybe that says something about you," he said blandly. I could sense him looking off into the garden three floors below his condo. He always had to put one hand behind his ear to hear the fountain bubbling.

"You're the psychologist. What would that say about me?"

"It says you're still looking for validation. The ability to paint as well as someone better known than you makes you his equal. Just a guess."

"I don't like the sound of that; I thought I was doing OK at the easel as Paul Zacher. How much is this going to cost me?"

"Two grand. This guy puts out the word on the fourteen Matisses missing from the Nice Prefecture in

1944 to his usual clientele network. We won't know who they are, or where they are, and he's free of any potential charges of conspiracy, fraud, etc. We hold him harmless, I believe is the legal term, and if any transactions come out of it, he gets 15%. He's going to trust us on that. Maybe we can snag Glass on this too for some rap in the States. We'll see how it goes."

"I can see there's a lot of trust going around here," I said. "What's your gut feeling on it?"

"I like it. I put it together myself, mostly, with your money. How bad can the guy be? He loves art. That's your usual position, anyway. I guess you're not saying that about Glass, though."

"So, what happens when the hook is set?"

"Glass—if it is Glass—contacts Gerson, and he forwards the message to me at my very anonymous email address. I could be anyone, anywhere. Then I'll send Gerson high-resolution jpegs of your two Matisses and tell him that if we can do a successful deal on those, then we'll talk about the other twelve. Like it's a test of good faith. When he responds after sending them to the client and establishing interest, we'll take a look at how he wants to do it, and then we set it up. The sweet thing is that at some point he's going to have to look at the paintings in the flesh, so to speak, and then we've got him. Even if I have to sit down with Glass in person, it's fine—he's never seen me before. I can talk art pretty well, if you give me some basics."

"What's the back story? It'll have to explain why these fourteen paintings are in México. We need him busted here."

"I thought about that. If we get that far, we can

say they came into Haiti after the War, because that's a French-speaking territory, and now because of political instability there, the owner has brought them into México. Haiti's just a hop away, and I wouldn't think we'd need any detail beyond that. It would be natural on our part to not want to say too much more about it."

"That sounds good," I said. "Haiti's always unstable, and the owner might reasonably have fled France with the paintings after the defeat of the Germans to avoid giving them back to Matisse. The painter didn't die until 1954."

The taste of victory was starting to accumulate behind my tongue like some wonderfully pure narcotic of a kind normally beyond the budget of obscure painters. The best thing about it was that Glass would appreciate exactly the same aspect of the deal that I did—no one in France had ever seen these paintings. Getting hold of them was like a world-class exclusive. Within a select group, it would trumpet the fact that Glass knew more than anyone—no one still alive, anyway. I assumed the prefect from Nice was dead, and we didn't care where the real pictures were, since we were working hard to keep it all so private. Whoever had them had shown no sign of putting them on the market in all that time. Why would he now? Their reappearance would have caused a sensation, but then the Matisse estate would immediately come after him. His son had been an art dealer and other family members were still connected in the trade. It made me think that the paintings had either been destroyed, or the person who now had them didn't know what they were. It seemed hard to believe they'd so thoroughly disappeared, but it wasn't our problem. Only the fact that they were so deeply hidden made this ruse possible.

"Let's do it," I said. "I'll start blocking out the first one tomorrow. Then I'll call Fidelity and get the money transferred. But wait a minute; what if it's not Glass who responds to this feeler from Gerson, the 'retired' art fence?"

"I asked them about that. It's the single detail they got out of him—Bernhard Glass was one of Gerson's clients. I'm sure it'll be him. Of course, he won't want to identify himself any more than we will."

I could see this coming together so perfectly it was almost immoral. Now that I had gone back over my history with him, I felt I knew Bernhard Glass thoroughly. He wouldn't be able to resist this deal. It was payback time for seven cardboard boxes of plywood and one girlfriend kidnapped across international borders. I had to smile, because, truthfully, I almost felt sorry for the man. He was in over his massive head.

Yet that in itself should have suggested caution to me, but somehow it didn't. After all, I'm an optimist. Although I also understand that what you don't learn the first time through, you still learn later, only at a much higher cost. In that regard, experience is much like an auction.

CHAPTER 11

I was tempted to wear my beret at a rakish angle as I worked on the Matisses. Practically single-handed he had originated the smock and beret look, the ultimate cliché of the mid twentieth-century painter. But I didn't. I wore my usual battered jeans and an old plaid cotton shirt with a frayed collar.

Maya came into the studio as I was cleaning up from the session.

"How many of the saint reproductions have you done?"

"Three."

"I have an idea. You're going to deliver them to your collector in Guadalajara, right?"

"Once they're dry. They're almost there now. Maybe in another day I could pack them." I use a fast drying medium.

"Then why don't we look at the Virgin of Guadalupe? It's on tour now for the first time ever. It'll be there in Guadalajara soon. It was the new pope's idea, that German guy. The Vatican is financing it."

I couldn't believe she was saying this.

"Don't tell me you never saw it in México City—you grew up there."

"I didn't have a chance. My family hated the

Church, remember?"

"They didn't let you?"

"It never came up. It was like it didn't exist. It almost seemed to embarrass them. Later, when I was in college, I didn't have time to think about it."

"You never even went to see it on a school trip?"

"It was a school for people who didn't want the religious stuff in their children's classrooms."

I guess with twenty million people, México City was big enough to have specialized schools of that kind.

"And I suppose the shopping is good in Guadalajara?"

"Of course. Much better than here. It's a real place. With all the expatriates, this is getting to be more like a Latino suburb of Gringolandia. And you're going to be collecting some money for those pictures, right?"

"We do enjoy Guadalajara. My customer always pays up front. But for you this is mostly about seeing the Virgin?"

"Call it partly. Don't you want to see it? I'm curious about it now."

"Why not? I have some ideas about what it is, and they're not what the public thinks," I said.

"And I have some ideas about what it isn't. It'll be perfect. I know this charming bed and breakfast."

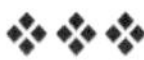

Maya shot the finished Matisses with our new Nikon D60, front and back. We thought the buyer would want to be sure they weren't painted on a piece of new linen fresh off the roll. I emailed the four images to Cody.

I thought the paintings looked good, although short of Matisse's best work of the period. Since they weren't copies, but inventions on a theme by Henri Matisse, I might have gotten into his head a bit deeper if I'd had more time and more insight. But he had the beginnings of his health issues during that time, and by the early years of the war, he was uneven himself as he worked. I'm not making excuses, but to be equal to his best, you really had to be him on a good day. I'm sure he aspired to that as well, and like me, he didn't always hit the very top of his form. Still, I'd like to see him try to do a Paul Zacher, who on his best day, can be hard to beat.

When Matisse died toward the end of 1954, he was just short of his eighty-fifth birthday, so I had tried to paint like he was sixty-five—mature, insightful, and still fairly nimble.

I had to admit, though, that he'd never been reduced to copying seventeenth-century devotional pictures for a deeply religious collector in Guadalajara. I was reminded of what Cody had said about my need for validation. These insights that he occasionally came up with might explain why I've never dated a psychologist.

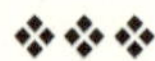

Three days later Cody received a forwarded email from a person who signed himself Botticelli. A lovely name, evocative of the great Renaissance painter who had a thing for strawberry blond girls dancing half-clothed within a springtime glade. It could have been a coincidence, but it didn't look like one to me. The sender's email address gave nothing away. I was running errands and I had stopped by Cody's condo to see how we were doing. We sat out on his narrow balcony, overlooking the marginal communal garden three floors below.

"Botticelli," he said, wanted to see images of the two Mattisses, and to learn their provenance.

"You mean he wants to know where they were stolen from?" I said, aghast.

"I guess."

"Why would we give that away? I think it's a dumb question. And why would ethics matter to him? As one of the great art thieves of our era, why would Glass think he could even ask that? I'm insulted. It sounds like he thinks we're minor league, or he's trying to come on like some great legitimate collector."

"I think it's dumb too," said Cody, "but he's the client here. Or maybe it's only a feeler from Interpol, and Glass isn't in this at all. Somehow they picked up the thread. They might be watching Gerson too."

"Maybe this buyer is imagining we don't really have all fourteen of them yet, and he might be able to steal the rest himself if he can get us to tell him where they are. Like we're that stupid—but that would be exactly the arrogance of Glass."

"OK, here's what we do." Cody paused to knock back a long snort of his planter's punch. "We pull in our horns a little here, since we've got some time. Maybe we're not as eager as he is, or we might have other people interested too, and we're weighing their merits as buyers.

What's the risk to us? In any case, we don't respond right away. Let him stew for a while. If it is Glass, he can't bear being ignored, right? You knew him well."

"I did, but can we risk that?" I asked. "Maybe he'll walk away."

"It's a negotiation. They're never all smooth and easy, OK? We're feeling our way through it. The key is to be quick on our feet."

"You've done this before, so you believe nimble sometimes means doing nothing?"

"I've had hostage training. It was all simulation with experts."

"Then the kidnappers weren't real."

"Of course not."

"Did you ever get a real hostage freed?"

"No. Did you ever fool anyone with a fake Matisse you'd painted yourself before? Or two? And they're not even hardly dry yet?"

"No."

"Alright. Cut me some slack here. We're both winging it. This can work if you let it."

I decided to swing with his experience and just wait. Twenty-four hours later another message came in from Botticelli, forwarded by Gerson. This time he made no mention of provenance, so we thought we'd show some flexibility ourselves as a goodwill gesture. Take a little, give a little.

"Let's feed him the Haiti story," I said. "It's just goofy enough to be plausible, and it'll help explain why the Matisses are in México."

"But not in San Miguel."

"Which we'll never mention. I'm sure Glass can't

stand the name of the town anymore. Let's say they're in Guadalajara. I've got to go there anyway to deliver three devotional pictures for my religious tequila king, Vidal Almeida. Maya has some things on her list. Why not come along and we'll bust Glass too? I'll pack the Matisses with the devotionals. You can be the front man on that deal, since nobody knows you."

Cody passed the Haiti story on to Botticelli. He'd had time to elaborate it a bit, and he suggested that the fourteen confiscated paintings had for a while been in the collection of Doc Duvalier and later, that of his son, Baby Doc. When Baby Doc suddenly had to flee to France after his ouster from Haiti in the eighties, he was traveling light. The difficult provenance of the paintings also made it imprudent for Baby Doc to take them back into France. After all, the boat was already overladen with premium rum and gold bullion. Art was a lesser priority.

That ultimately put them in play once again. I thought this had the enticing feel of insider information, a species of knowledge irresistible to Glass because of its exclusivity. It was in his nature to never share.

"You're good," I said to Cody. "You're getting a real knack for art fraud. That's the kind of line he'll love. He'll think he's in there mixing it up with the heavy hitters."

Cody emitted a mild snort. "He is."

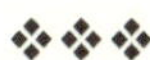

Five days later I called Delgado and told him,

confidentially, that we'd heard Bernhard Glass was going to be in Guadalajara, and we were going there to track him down if we could. I offered no more detail. Delgado gave me the name of a prosecutor in the local judicial police, and said he'd call ahead for us. If we located Glass, they'd pick him up and hold him for Delgado. How hard could this be? If we couldn't prove my old art professor was behind the murder of the thief, Carlos Ortíz, the man who'd taken the real la Tour out of the Bellas Artes show, then we'd get him for the kidnapping of Maya, since the crime had happened in San Miguel. The next morning we loaded the new artmobile with my three fake devotionals and Matisses and headed for México's second largest city.

We had Maya's laptop aboard so Cody could maintain contact with Botticelli once we arrived. We were all in high spirits, for a variety of reasons. Maya was going to get Glass busted, without having to kill him herself; Cody was the point man in a carefully managed ruse; and I was going to deliver to Bernhard Glass a comeuppance he wouldn't have thought possible in his worst nightmares.

"What are they worth?" said Cody as we crossed the state border into Jalisco. It was red earth tequila country, with rolling kilometers of blue-green agave poking their lethal spines toward the sun. From the roasted root boles of these plants, tequila was fermented. It was one of the two lubricants that kept México running; the other was petroleum. You could light a match to either of them.

"The new Matisses? If they were real and could be legally sold at auction, I would think three to six million dollars each. It partly depends on the stock market whether people are feeling wealthy at a given moment."

"How much do we ask for them, then?" said Maya. If she'd had a calculator, she would have had it in hand, her nails chattering across the keys.

"Maybe 10%? Or, how about a million for the pair? Glass could afford that, with all the loot he's pulling in from sales of the genuine paintings he's stolen. We don't want to price them so high that he backs off. You've got to remember that he's not used to paying for what he gets, aside from operating costs. On the other hand, if they're too cheap, he'll think they're fakes."

"You're going to enjoy this, aren't you?" Cody looked at me like I was having too much fun.

"Absolutely."

"So we could do some serious shopping here," Maya said, thoughtfully. "They make wonderful furniture and they'll ship anywhere. That sofa in the great room is getting kind of ratty. Plus, I wouldn't mind going to Italy one of these years. There's a hotel in Venice where the gondola delivers you right to your door."

"Don't forget we've got to give Gerson a 15% commission," said Cody.

"Look," I said, "we're not going to make any deals, we're only going to bust Glass. That's it. He's not going to have the cash in his pocket anyway. The best case is that we'll get him to a meeting to inspect the two pictures, and the guy from the judicial cops will be there as well to take him away in cuffs. That's all."

"So it'll be another Boy Scout case. Why am I not surprised?" Maya said, in a tone that made it sound more like Tenderfoot than Eagle Scout. "We do our good deed, hang out in the background with no glory because it all has to be confidential, and when it's finished, nobody pays us. That's like our last case, where saving Governor Sanz was going to get us sashes with emeralds and public honors. I'm just trying to pay the bills here, OK? While you guys float around Harry's running up the bar bill and signing autographs for single women."

"We're mostly there to hand out business cards," said Cody.

"Well, we didn't save Sanz, did we? He was gunned down twenty minutes after he left us. Anyway, this case has been like that the whole time, ever since I noticed that the *St. Jerome* in the VRC show was real. The only money that's going to change hands in this one is from the three devotional pictures—seven thousand dollars. I'll contribute it to the agency for overhead."

"Don't you usually get more than that for three pictures?" said Cody. "Not that your offer isn't generous and accepted with gratitude by the staff."

"You're the staff," said Maya. "I'm the director."

"Yes, I do get more," I said, "but no gallery is involved in this deal to take a cut. I gave the collector a break because he contacted me directly. This is his third purchase."

"Who is he?" asked Maya.

"His name is Vidal Almeida. He's a big deal in the tequila business. No surprise there, but you won't see his name on any bottles. He buys in barrels from small producers on ranchos that don't have their own facilities for marketing and distribution. Then he bottles it under several different labels depending on the quality and the aging. You've probably drunk one of his blends without knowing it."

"But he lives in town, in Guadalajara?" said Maya. "Why is that?"

"He's got a big house there, in the Tlaquepaque neighborhood, and a ranch with the production facility further out toward the city of Tequila. It's not that far away."

"Then he must have his own chapel," said Cody, "like on a hacienda."

"He does. These three pictures I did for him will go on the back wall. He told me that once they're hung, worshipers will look up at them as they leave. He asked me if I had any ideas for a grand altarpiece, but I had to say I didn't. I told him if he came up with something I could probably copy it. Then later, he said he'd found the perfect thing, but it wasn't a copy. For that close to the altar, *to God's house on earth*, as he said, he'd decided he didn't want to use a reproduction. I got the impression that he may have located something in Spain that was in a condition that met his standards. Sometimes if a church falls on hard times they're forced to sell off their altarpiece just to pay the bills."

"The Church is in trouble there, too," said Maya.

"Everywhere," I said. "Even in México."

CHAPTER 12
NATTY BOLLANDER

Because Natty had a shorter time frame to produce his current masterpiece on location, he'd chosen acrylics as his medium. They dried thoroughly overnight, and while under UV light they were detectable as different from oils, the nature of the project suggested that this painting would never be exposed to it. The Church maintained that the surface of the Our Lady of Guadalupe image had not been painted at all. The official line was that the pigment was a supernatural material, not susceptible to scientific analysis. It was in their power to invite another detailed scientific scrutiny, but they hadn't in years. Besides, what else might a UV examination reveal? Nothing that the Church would want known. Natty, for whom shortcuts were not unfamiliar, felt comfortable with this; the condition he most desired in life.

When he thought he was finished with the Our Lady of Guadalupe reproduction, he took half an hour to perform his standard final inspection. He removed it from its taped position on the wall and rehung it upside down. Next to it he hung the print he'd worked from upside down as well. That was the critical test. He walked to the opposite end of the room and fixed his eyes on the images, switching back and forth, moving closer step by step detail by detail. Varying distances gave him different information. All of it was good.

As he painted it, Natty had increasingly felt it was intended primarily as a decorative picture: the repetitive elements of the original were key. He found it easy to copy, because the seventeenth century artist who painted it was not sophisticated about his concept. It was all about the recurring themes in the Virgin's aura. Repetition was the principal element. Natty knew the concept well; he saw it in things like embroidery, beadwork, jewelry; any design that involved symmetry and a texture made up of many small elements in series. This was why fish scales were beautiful when still on the fish, but not when removed.

It was no more sophisticated than beating a drum, and he quickly caught the rhythm of the image. Natty understood it so well, he was soon holding himself back as he painted it. He saw additional ways to embellish the design, strokes that would have improved it.

Chiara came in as he went through his final point-for-point examination. At that point he was on his knees, three feet away from the pictures.

"I didn't know you were religious," she said, standing next to him. Her eyes followed his.

"I paint illusion. Religion is illusion. It suits me fine. It's no different from anything I do, since I understand it."

"You do have your comfort zone."

"Doesn't everyone?"

"What will you work on next?"

"Whatever is needed, I don't know."

"So the idea doesn't come from you?"

Natty turned his head to the side and looked at

her for the first time. An irritated frown pushed the corners of his mouth downward. This was too close to an uncomfortable truth. "Let me finish this now. I need to concentrate. This is the most important part." He focused on the face of the image. Up or down, in either position it looked pinched and graceless. The skin tones were ambiguously dark, although the features were European. Was this done to connect to the indigenous Méxicans? Now Natty was thinking that the painting hadn't been done in Spain, but in México to provide an artifact specifically to support the legend.

"So much effort that is," Chiara said, her arms folded, "to make one thing exactly like another. To check it back and forth; a little here, a little there." Her head wobbled from side to side as if she were dizzy. "Most painters would want to make their work unique, not to be like a human copy machine. Who buys this?"

Natty paused for a moment. He sensed a tone in her voice he didn't remember hearing before, but it was the wrong moment for a serious discussion. He wasn't finished with his inspection. Perhaps it couldn't be avoided.

"Dr. Glass is the customer." Usually he had concealed from her the Skirra reproductions that he worked from in his studio in Florence, allowing her to see only the finished pictures. He didn't want to know whether she recognized that all his paintings were copies or not. It hadn't come up in their conversations; and they had never before come this close to it. He didn't encourage her to talk about art. In the past, her occasional comments on the subject suggested that she understood nothing about it anyway. Working now in the close quarters of their hotel room, no such ruse was possible anymore. Although their nights were still occasionally magical, Natty realized he didn't care to have Chiara around all the time, especially during working hours. It was always a relief in the morning when she went off to her job at the insurance agency. He missed his privacy, and he'd instinctively known for a long time that he could never marry her. Because she never brought it up anymore, he thought she understood that now too.

"The Dr. Glass, he has bought other pictures? Other copies like this?"

Natty gave up the detailed scan of the Virgin's face, specifically the opaque blackness of her pupils. No ghost images were present in the Skirra print; he'd scanned it with a magnifying glass he brought from Florence. Glass's name would mean nothing to Chiara. Otherwise Natty would've made something else up. On the other hand, this conversation, while a long time in coming, had perhaps always been inevitable. At least, he'd always dreaded its arrival.

"He's bought a few. Here, sit down with me, darling." He led her to one of the chairs flanking the window and took the other himself. He would have taken her hand as he spoke, but they were too far apart. From there, he could still scan the new painting for gross errors as they talked. "Dr. Glass is a sophisticated collector, a scholar of art. He's the head of an important institution that studies fakes. Yes, fakes! Because we can all learn from them." Natty nodded confidentially. "I see that you're surprised. He's hired me a number of times in the past to illustrate how a fake of a given painting could be done. It's a kind of demonstration, you know? His work is educational, and he uses these examples in his lectures.

He could show slides, I suppose, like some experts do, but the physical example will demonstrate the brushwork, the nuances of color—the really subtle things about a fake. He even lets his students touch them. You've probably seen that I never sign some of them."

The truth was that he signed most of them, but never with his own name. Relieved at the explanation, he unintentionally exhaled broadly. Natty was proud of himself for spontaneously hitting upon an explanation that was almost true. Like the work he did with his brush, it landed somewhere between plausible and convincing. It contained about 94% truth—as close as you could come to purity in anything, even better than jewelry silver. He thought of it as being like an alloy. After all, eighteen karat gold was only three-quarters pure, and the rest was usually copper. How much more could a person demand than that? Natty's world was one of approximation; he inched ever closer to an unreachable perfection. In the end, the only thing that counted was being closer than anyone else, close enough to be undetectable, even by experts. This was what Dr. Glass was paying for.

Chiara didn't respond immediately; her face remained sober and unmoved. Natty suddenly wondered if Dr. Glass—whom he privately thought of as the man with the muffin-top neck—had made a well-meaning mistake when he invited Chiara along on this trip. Glass could be generous too, when things were going his way, which was most of the time. On Natty's semiannual visits to London, Glass also produced first class Cuban cigars—not the typical Monte Cristo torpedoes and Cohibas that everyone overpaid for on a February lark in the Caribbean, but the private-label masterpieces rolled from an obscure but noble leaf in Oriente province, one that Glass claimed not even Fidel had discovered. Naturally, they were not officially exported, and the VRC director served a breath-taking cognac with them often, distilled in minute batches by a small producer in France that practically no one had heard of. These receptions made Natty wonder whether Glass had come from nothing, since he appeared to be obsessed with knowing what no one else knew. The role of the ultimate insider is best played by someone who began life as a complete outsider. When the director told him what these cigars cost, suddenly it all became too much about display. Natty pictured himself smoking rolled-up twenty-pound notes, more than one at a time. Why would Dr. Glass tell him this, except to glorify himself and underline his generosity?

"So, the next picture you paint goes to him too?" Chiara said, interrupting these thoughts after a long silence. "The doctor, I mean."

She's back on point, Natty thought, after all that. The insurance business must have given her a linear mind. I should tell her less, not more.

"If he asks for it. Who knows?" Glass had already talked to him about doing a little-known Franz Hals when he got back to Florence. After three generations in a private collection in Antwerp, Skirra didn't have that one either, so there would be a problem getting it right.

"You have no certainty in this business?" Chiara said with a look of surprise.

"What artist has any? Did Leonardo, Rafael, Caravaggio have certainty?"

"Well…" Accustomed to the certainty of actuarial tables in her office, Chiara's hands fluttered with doubt.

"Rubens, Bosch, van Gogh, Picasso?" He could have gone on, but Natty stopped and waited for her response.

"Well, Picasso, I think, yes, didn't he?"

"Too much, for my taste. He could do anything he wanted, so he got lazy and repeated himself endlessly."

"But I think you can do anything. I have seen you. "

This was not the response Natty wanted, so he said, facing her, "I have no painting style of my own."

Chiara stared at him blankly. "But I think you have *every* style. I have seen many of them. Who could be the equal of you?"

"You don't understand. To have every style is to have none. It is like being a great stage actor: when the performance is over, you remove your makeup and hang up your costume, you put on your nondescript street clothes, and as you slip out the stage door, you are once again no one. In your heart, you are anonymous. You are famous, but people do not recognize you in the street." Natty shook his head. This was the most truthful statement he'd ever made to her, and, if she still didn't get it, he couldn't elaborate it any further. Shaking his head, he walked into the bathroom to clean his brushes. He felt like he was hanging up his costume. The canvas was finished, and in his heart, even though the painting of the virgin was unsigned, Natty no longer knew who he was.

Later, he checked his email messages on his laptop and sent one off to Dr. Glass in return. "Your prayers are answered today. I'll see you in Guadalajara with the great lady who is our mutual friend."

CHAPTER 13

I don't need to detail the drive into Guadalajara. It begins with a hundred miles of rolling high desert, dotted with scrubby mesquite and prickly pear cactus. Mountains guard the horizon. The earth grows redder with what must be a higher level of iron. Gradually the agaves begin to appear. Soon they're cultivated in rows. Imagine 150 miles of those lethal soldiers clawing their way out of red sand. Setting up to spear anything that passes, they make great fences when planted. Guadalajara itself begins to make you crazy with anticipation when you're still about ten miles out. What awaits you, as you're sucked bodily into the traffic, is having your poise stripped away, and your hands leaving sweaty streaks on the wheel. You are a gladiator in your car.

"How are you doing?" asked Maya. She'd been quiet for a while.

"I'm good."

"Want me to drive?" said Cody.

"It's OK."

"Let me know if you change your mind." Once in the steel talons of the traffic, it would no longer be possible to change my mind. I wanted to stay behind the wheel because I knew where we were going, approximately. I understood Tlaquepaque when I found it.

We hadn't heard back yet from Botticelli, so our plan was to deliver the three devotionals to Vidal Almeida and collect for them, meanwhile hoping to make contact with Botticelli on the fake Matisses. The ball was in his court, and on his own schedule. We could hang around for a while, but we couldn't force him to email us. We literally had no idea where in the world he was, but Cody had made it clear that the Matisses were in Guadalajara, if he wanted to examine them. I was starting to believe this was chancier than we'd thought. What if Glass simply wouldn't be lured out of the U.S. or London for anything?

Vidal Almeida's mansion was in the heart of Tlaquepaque, an old village that had been absorbed by the outward advance of the city of Guadalajara early in the last century. It lay in the southeast corner. I had sent him high-resolution shots of the three devotional pictures, and he'd approved them. I'd met him only once, at the time of our first deal. I expected this transaction would probably be handled by his representative, since the tequila baron already knew the quality of my work. His polite but still terse communications suggested he was a busy man with many demands on his time.

Although the density and speed of the traffic can sometimes cause my teeth to curl, getting out of Guadalajara is much more difficult than getting in. It's like hell in that respect, because the exit route is not well marked once you're inside it, even though you more or less knew how you got there in the first place. It may stem from an assumption that once in Guadalajara, you wouldn't want to leave. I didn't mind the place, but I preferred the scale of San Miguel, at 75,000 people, instead of four and a half million who were bent on running each other down.

Still, I found my way into the more tranquil village of Tlaquepaque without incident, but I was still working to smooth out the knotted muscles along the edge of my jaw with my fingertips.

I had made my first sale to Almeida nearly three years before. I never knew how he found out about me, but he had ordered a copy of a small *tondo* (circular format) by Raphael from the Vatican Museum. It was just under eleven inches in diameter. He had seen it in Rome twice, once immediately after a personal audience with the Holy Father, and was ecstatic about it. It bore the face of a cherub, and the frame had no space for the wings, so it might have been only a mischievous little boy with rosy cheeks and a Hollywood haircut.

Almeida had found a great print of it for me to work from. It looked like it had been cut from an archival book. Although it was no epic project, initially I'd found the task daunting, being the work of Raphael, a painter far more formidable than Georges de la Tour. Small scale doesn't mean easy; often it's the opposite. There's no room for error. But I figured if it didn't succeed, he could reject it. Nothing would be lost. Even better, that would show me my current limits, which I always find useful to know. That's what sets up my next goal. In this case the task was to wrap my mind around what Raphael had done, not only in concept, but brushstroke by brushstroke, because, from long practice, I knew that the ability to create a true reproduction came from *understanding* the picture you're copying. The physical skills are secondary to that.

Almeida had already found a circular frame for it, or had one made. You can find people in México who can fabricate anything. There were times when I thought this included every-day reality. In the States, most people believe the old skills have died, so they usually don't even bother to look for them. But they haven't—they've only moved to México, like I have. Of course, that's not true; they never fell out of use here—it's a different mindset; one that embraces continuity as an alternative to progress. That's one of the things I like best about it. After my time here, when I go back to the States I feel like I'm in a foreign country. Absence makes the heart grow, not fonder, but off on a different path.

Painting that picture gave me new respect for the delicacy of Raphael's touch. Even though he could work brilliantly on large-scale frescos, he still retained the tenderness of a lover and the plausibility of an adulterer on the more intimate scale of small canvases. When I delivered it, concealing my pride, because I knew I had nailed it, Almeida went for it in a big way, although he didn't shout or wave his arms. We each had a glass of exquisite champagne as I sat on his terrace overlooking a broad, sun-soaked garden, centered by an enormous fountain. It looked like the antechamber to heaven.

He was a large man for a Méxican, but trim, with big shoulders and the required mustache. Naturally, his skin was as pale as mine. That day he wore a tan suit with a darker bar over the back collar, and a string tie. His boots were exquisitely embroidered—I can see them still. For a major figure in his industry, he didn't strike me as overbearing or excessively commanding, and his voice sounded surprisingly soft and cultivated while we talked about painting, a subject on which he was well informed. Almeida quickly got to the point as he questioned me at length on how it felt to be able to reproduce a Raphael using nothing more than my own hands and eyes. He said he couldn't imagine it, and since painting it is a right-brain kind of thing, the nonverbal side of mental effort, I could hardly describe it to him, either. No words had gone into the making of it. I was more able to describe the feeling of doing it than the process. When still on the easel, Maya had fallen hard for it and wanted to keep it for our bedroom, but I couldn't bring myself to make another one. It would have been too much like starting an assembly line.

Of course, my conversation with Almeida was all in Spanish. As he spoke I thought that when he gave orders, you would instinctively lean closer to him and listen carefully. I guessed his age at not far from fifty, but which side it fell on, I couldn't have said.

When he made a second set of purchases a year later, one of his drivers picked them up from me in San Miguel, so I hadn't seen him since. While I never thought we could be friends, I valued his respect for my ability, since he was a connoisseur. Even so, no number of champagne flutes could have gotten out of me the secret of reproducing a Rafael. I simply didn't know how to say it in words. I could more easily have guided Almeida's own untutored hand over the canvas.

Now we were cruising down Cruz Verde toward Independencia in Tlaquepaque. Neither Maya nor Cody had been there before. Maya had found us an attractive bed and breakfast on the Internet that she remembered hearing about from a friend.

"Upscale," said Cody, looking down both sides of the street at the intersection. "Probably no sports bars here, I guess." He sighed.

"You travel like this, you're going to pay a certain

price," I said. "Where you go is not ever going to be home, except at the very end."

"But you could come shopping with me," said Maya, brightly, (I never did, except for groceries) with a certain smoldering quality I recognized with some degree of nostalgia. "I know you can get the American bras here. They have good lift (to her, leeft), not that I need any. But I have to think of the future, the far *distant* future." I saw her hand come forward from the back seat as she reached up and pressed two cool fingers to Cody's lower cheek, as if taking his pulse; an unsubtle gesture. I thought I knew what that pulse rate would be, but Maya handled triple digits well. Nor did her eyelids need any lift as they fluttered in Cody's direction.

"At your service." If Cody could have bowed in my van without hitting his head on the dash, he would have. The passenger seat in front was the only one that accommodated him. This was nothing short of torture, but I think Maya was bored by the four-hour drive, and in that condition, she could become subtly sadistic. She only thought of it as dangerous, and to her, dangerous was a plus in any woman. Modest, submissive, and quiet were not in her vocabulary.

I briefly glanced at him while he searched for any further response to this. It was too intimate and visual for him. In his situation, there was none that I could've come up with, either. Cody had been in love with her for a long time. It didn't bother me, but Maya had always known it and enjoyed egging him on. Furthermore, I knew that in my absence they had a more intimate style of exchange; the differences were probably not meaningful, only more fun. Sex is always on the table here, no matter who sits in the chairs.

As I had realized early on about Maya, her flirting mechanism would be the last thing to go, as her vital signs shut down one by one in her final hour. She was typical of many México women in this respect. Had there been a flirting event in the México City Olympics in 1968, (a puzzling oversight; it would have greatly boosted the home team medal count) Maya, had she been old enough to be there, (she wasn't even born then) would've medalled in broad jump, pole vault, breaststroke, and hundred-yard flash—her running shorts being far briefer than most. She would have passed on anything with relays—she preferred the effort to be exclusively under her control. Nobody does it better—she had the ability to beckon to you with one hand even as she held you at arm's length with the other. In his position as Distant Admirer #1, this was what Cody was constantly faced with. If he hadn't enjoyed her attention so much, I might have felt sorry for him.

"Here's the house," I said, not sad to cut short this foreplay. "Look at that! I could live there in a heartbeat."

The mansion of Vidal Almeida looked like the goal of Renaissance design, and that of every century thereafter. At least it summed up those styles better than any art survey course at the Metropolitan Museum. Looking at it again in daylight, after several years, I felt that Vidal Almeida had understood completely what he was about, and he'd had the sense to let someone of great wealth and taste build it for him 110 years before he was born.

It covered half the long block going each way from the intersection of Independencia and Cruz Verde. The mansion was, from its design, mid 1800s. The delicate, but authoritative hand of French design in this period elaborated every detail. It was painted a pale, dry shade of yellow, with white trim at the windows, doors, and cornices. Over each window was a half-round pediment. On the roofline, an elegant baluster was topped by grand finials as big as tureens. At the intersection, the mansion had a tall second-floor room, matched by another down Independencia on the right corner of the principal block. The main floor was high enough without them—I remembered from my champagne toast with Vidal Almeida that the ceilings on the main floor were about twenty feet high. Guadalajara possesses a warmer climate than San Miguel, and the afternoon heat was meant to collect up under the ceiling. Here it had ample opportunity.

The front entrance doors, which I had used on my first visit, were about fifteen feet tall, ending in an arch with a carved keystone. They were three panels high, each one ornately carved with a large rosette in the center. The hardware was a cast bronze handle like an upright spiral baton in brackets on each one, with a high-security modern lockset above and below on the left member of the pair. The cast bronze key plate was finished to match the entry handles.

Beyond at the right, the mansion ended in a carriage wing fronted by five tall arches with grills. The interior at that end was now a garden facing the street. It was too public for family. On the Cruz Verde side, the first floor wall was mostly blank. The street sloped downward to Juarez, and near the far end of the mansion, a carriage opening framed a set of rusted steel entry doors of great character, studded and barred. The rust was an intentional and visually effective finish. Uniform in color, it echoed the way you might make a sculpture in Cor-Ten steel for a public plaza in the States. But these doors looked more formidable than artistic. You'd need a tank to get through them if they weren't open to you. As we approached and slowed, giving them room to swing toward us, a single camera eye rotated in our direction without blinking, and when I turned farther onto the apron, the steel doors opened outward to welcome us. I had expected to show my credentials before we got to this point, but I suddenly sensed that I already had done that without knowing it.

That we were dealing with a level of technology beyond most private homes still did not bother me. Although I hadn't met them, I assumed Vidal Almeida had family as well as his collections to protect—a serious business. In México, kidnapping can be an issue more painful than theft. What was disturbing to me was that the security camera, and the system behind it, appeared to recognize my van. Or was it my cheerful face framed in the windshield? Was the camera mapping the detail of my irises? I tried not to blink.

Still, I rolled right in. Business is often done on a handshake here, and I had several times shaken the manicured hand of Vidal Almeida. I felt I must have been programmed into his security apparatus in a general way, but how did he know my van? I'd replaced it since I last dealt with him.

"What the hell!" said Cody. "Isn't that the damnedest security system? Maybe it knows your license number. This guy is ingenious."

"Makes me feel welcome and uncomfortable at the same time," said Maya. "But I feel like I don't know what I'm showing him. It's like the airport security in the States. If his system is showing me naked, maybe I should strike a pose."

"Maybe if you'd worn a different bra," I said, knowing I'd pay for that later.

"Do you think they can see me in the back seat?"

We came to rest just inside the doors, and they closed behind us without a sound. Whatever we were there for, we weren't going to leave without paying for it, or distributing it. On the left, I could have turned into a space for four cars. Two stalls were open, and the other two held identical white Suburbans. One of them had a vanity license plate—something I don't see often here. It read, *Agave*—the critical component of tequila.

A small, uniformed man appeared at my elbow, waving me to a stop. The gesture was at once authoritative and polite. He had no need to pull out the automatic pistol on his belt. A uniformed guard waited against the wall on each side of us. Neither of them looked at the van. The fact that we had entered so easily vouched for us.

The Almeida livery that all three wore was gray and informal; it looked paramilitary without being militant. The message was *private* security. With their emphasis on being discreet, they weren't likely to break up a confrontation out on the street unless it was edging uncomfortably toward the house. The small man opened the doors for each of us, then came around to the driver's door last.

"I am called Armando. Sr. Almeida will be with you in a moment." He said this in English.

We waited at an ornate grilled opening that faced a broad garden. The center was dominated by a squared-circle fountain in the Moorish style that must have been thirty feet across. Near each of the four corners of the square stood a sculpture. The one nearest us was a cross about twenty feet high, all four members intricately carved with what might have been a network of snakes. One or two tequilas too many and they'd appear to be writhing. I remembered from my prior visit that above us was a long *loggia* facing the garden. It turned the corner at the bottom and continued overhead to the far end, facing the back of the greater part of the house. As we looked out, on the right, where the garden ended, a flight of steps led up to the broad covered terrace where I'd sat drinking champagne with Almeida two years before. The tequila baron was descending these steps as I watched.

While Maya liked men of a certain status in general, Vidal Almeida was the kind of man she especially appreciated. He was rich, powerful, good-looking, and in his prime. I don't disparage myself, but he was the kind of man who could make me wonder just a little how she'd ended up with me. He was wearing jeans with a crease, a white western-cut shirt, and a suede jacket with a patch on the right shoulder meant to receive the butt of a rifle. By the time he'd circled the end of the fountain and approached the ornate grill where we stood, I could see he was looking only at Maya. Of course, that's the Méxican manner.

Cody was looking at her too, but with an expression of dismay.

"Next he'll be commissioning me to do a portrait of you," I said to her quietly.

"Nude," Cody said, bluntly, and in a less accommodating tone.

Maya didn't react. I'd painted her nude nearly forty times, pictures that were dispersed from Buenos Aires to the Yukon. It wouldn't matter to her if Almeida bought the next one. She'd probably suggest it to him and offer a favorable price.

The small man in uniform stepped forward and unlocked the grill as Almeida approached. He shook hands cordially all around as we did the introductions, and he finished by commenting on my current show in Mérida, in the Yucatan, which greatly surprised me. He spoke of it in enough detail to convince me he'd really seen it, as he led us past the fountain along a stone walk at the edge of the lawn. It was called *Private Lives*, and it examined people doing what they candidly did in real life, posed to look unposed. A body-shop repairman grinding down a fender repair, the sparks illuminating his face; or my neighbor Chile Colorado at her computer working on one of her best-selling westerns.

"Yet, somehow you missed having a *jimador* in one of your pictures," Almeida said with a broad smile. This was the field worker who harvests the root boles of the agave to make tequila.

As we passed, a large black lab, seated, watched us calmly with his tongue dangling. His leash was loosely draped over the edge of a carved limestone urn nearby. The formality of Almeida's lifestyle was well defined, but it stopped short of perfection. I somehow sensed that this was intentional, like everything else he did.

At the top of the stairs, we were met by a houseboy in a white jacket and black slacks. He carried a tray of champagne flutes engraved with an elaborate A. I didn't mind a glass of champagne in the afternoon when I'm not painting, particularly when it could only be Dom Pérignon or Louis Roederer Cristal. I didn't have it often enough to be able to decide which this was. I chose my glass when the tray stopped in front of me, even as I was also studying an immense painting on the western wall of the covered terrace. It depicted Napoleon and Josephine in quite formal outfits—did we ever see them kicking back? It must have been eight feet by ten. If it was not by Jacques-Louis David, then it was by a copyist of epic ability. I'd never done a painting that large, and it hadn't been there on my previous visit. Working on that scale was almost like doing murals, and I'd never attempted that either.

"First," said Almeida, raising his glass before taking the merest of sips, "we meet again, *maestro* Zacher. I must show you a prize of my collection. One of many, of course." Offering his arm with a flourish to Maya, who didn't hesitate to take it, he led us to the far side of the terrace and through a broad arch. There we stood on a shallow balcony overlooking the small formal garden that faced Independencia. Behind us was a room attached to the chapel like a sacristy, the area where the priest would change into his vestments before saying mass. Covering two walls were antique crucifixes, some in gold and emeralds, alternating with others in crude, hammered iron. On the back wall was the correct cabinetry; built-in stacks of flat, long drawers. A strangely austere pewter crucifix hung over it, unlike the others, and different from any I'd ever seen. Across the room from it, a tall shallow niche with an arched top was let into a plain, unadorned wall that faced the front garden. Hung inside at eye level was my Raphael cherub. From the opposite wall over the cabinets, a single pin-spot lit the boy's seductive face. I had caught sight of the picture from the corner of my eye as I walked in, but waited to look at it last. It was dessert for the eye.

"What you are thinking is correct," said Almeida, raising an eyebrow. "Your painting came first. I had the niche cut into the wall to prepare a setting for it. Do you see that, my friend? In this special place, it is in the quiet position that only draws the eye of the expert. Others walk past and rush to look at the gold crucifixes, the chunky emeralds. They believe they have seen value, but it is too subtle for them, I think, but never for me."

His voice dropped as he said this. It was a great effect, as Almeida well knew. It brought the *tondo* painting into sharp focus, and reinforced the circular form. The blank wall moved the viewer's eye toward it from every direction. But was it a fake? If he saw it, Rafael would react with indignation, but it was not for me, the painter. My experience in painting it had been nearly as real as Raphael's. Unlike the la Tour, where I had ached to correct the poorly rendered eyes and hands as I copied it, I'd found nothing wanting in the work of the Renaissance master. I suddenly wished I could anonymously run it past Mr. Connoisseur, Dr. Bernhard Glass. I couldn't help but sigh. I wanted to talk about the experience of painting it, because in the time that had passed, I'd thought about it again many times, as if I still had the brush in my hand.

I glanced into the adjacent chapel. It was cruciform, and at the foot of the nave, the entry wall at the front was ready for my devotionals to go up in a row over the door. At the moment it held no seating, but I guessed that it might accommodate twenty people with no difficulty. Over the altar, the sanctuary wall was bare, as if cleared to receive the new altarpiece. I wondered what Almeida had found to display there, but I didn't feel I could ask. Although he would volunteer things at times, he was not a man you could casually question. Behind this exhibition of wealth and taste, I sensed his concern for privacy.

Back on the terrace, we found my three devotionals already unpacked and set along a wall for display. Almeida had given me free reign of subject, only specifying the approximate dimension that all of them would share. I had picked a St. Teresa in ecstasy, strongly Baroque in feeling, and suggestive of Bernini with his religious eroticism. He must have thought of heaven as an ongoing orgasm. For his Italian audience, that must have made sense. The second picture was a spare and haunted version of the three crosses on Golgotha, touched by a hint of surrealism. It was based on a little-known picture by Sandro Tolledano, and because it was not familiar, I'd taken a few liberties with it—one of the ways I kept my momentum going in pictures whose subject didn't interest me beyond the visuals. The last was a Palm Sunday picture of Christ on an ass, passing through a cheering crowd. Unlike most paintings of that subject, in this one he lacked a sappy expression on his face. I chose it because Christ's look was clouded with anticipatory sorrow, despite the crowd of adoring fans. Like a lot of pictures of that subject and era, it was mostly about fabric, and I do fabric well. People who love my nudes don't know this, and probably don't care.

Almeida walked back and forth in front of the three, pausing, leaning over to look closer at each one.

"Magnificent! Fresh, inspiring! The detail is exquisite! I so much prefer these to the originals." He grasped my right hand warmly, then studied it palm-upward as if it might reveal some secret skill that I hadn't divulged to him. Interacting with him carried a sense of intimacy that was merely temporary; you could be dismissed in an instant, no matter how profound you thought the connection.

I had excluded any hint of El Greco in this group, whose swishy pastel tones and draggy, hollow-cheeked brushwork leaves me cold. Almeida had given me the freedom to eliminate that transplanted painter, because when I took the job, I wanted to be sure he wasn't expecting it. Nor did I lust after the weepy saints of Murillo, although his brushwork was always impeccable.

"You are thinking, Señor Zacher, that the three crosses painting should be hung in the center, over the door?"

"Exactly," I said, "with the Santa Teresa on the right, Palm Sunday on the left. Think of it as chronological. I did as I worked on them. Perhaps the two flanking pictures could be slightly lower, reflecting their importance."

"You are an orderly person, for a painter, if I may say so. Structure is important to you. Let me also say that, from what I can see, you are a master. I thank you for that, as I'm sure others have before me."

Normally, after our experience with the agency, Maya would have contradicted the first clause of a statement like that. She felt that disorder, even chaos, hung in wreaths around my head, but this time she stayed silent, perhaps reluctant to contradict Almeida, who was now reaching again for her hand. Cody was largely silent through this, scanning the interiors as if they were a series of crime scenes.

All of our business was finished, so we moved back down toward the garden. After a formal goodbye, Almeida stayed behind on the terrace as we descended, and cordially waved to us as if from the bow of a ship about to disembark. It was not quite a princely wave, but nonetheless, one that suggested nobility and its privileges. He was moving on as we returned to our—not hovels, exactly, but next to this? What went on behind those long arched and private *loggias* we were passing? What wishes did the coins tossed into that great fountain solicit? I couldn't imagine what the Almeida family might lack, at a certain level. I glanced back as we walked. Other than staff, we'd seen no resident other than Vidal Almeida, although his presence was grand enough to fill the house. From his look, I thought he might have a harem back there, somewhere. Cody probably had the same thought. Maya didn't; she knew she was unique and was no candidate for anyone's harem. The grill at the car entry swung open as we approached, giving me the feeling that you didn't have to ask for anything there.

Suddenly, glancing along the wall that supported the *loggia* above, I saw among the rectangular, white stone pavers, glimpsed through a boxwood hedge, that alternate panels in the row were opaque glass. You would probably only notice this leaving, because, coming in your eye would be dominated by the magnificent terrace of the main house awaiting your arrival. Those glass panels could only mean one thing: another floor existed below. In Méxican Spanish, a sótano—a cellar. Why would Vidal Almeida need such a thing, when his above ground spaces were so compelling, so magnificent? Were the laundry and kitchen down there?

As we got back into the van, I studied the wall on the right, facing the parked cars. At the center it had a marble staircase with bronze sconce lights on both sides; a setting elegant enough for the family arriving home from the opera. Next to it was a simpler door. It might have opened upon a room for the security staff.

Armando, the small man in uniform, handed me the car keys and an envelope with a check in it. Without looking at it, I backed out onto Cruz Verde while one of the guards stopped traffic with a practiced gesture of his hand.

"That Almeida's a friendly guy," said Cody as the iron doors closed behind us, silently, but with a death grip.

"Very," said Maya. "Handsome, too. A connoisseur, obviously, and that's a plus." I couldn't see her, but I knew she was nodding.

"A connoisseur of many things," I said, "and some of them we can't even guess at. But why does a handsome, friendly connoisseur need a basement? Not for his plumbing, I would think. He's already got a warehouse for his tequila out in the country. Here, he must have a big art collection and climate-controlled vaults of images that he rotates around on his walls when the light is right."

"I suspect," said Cody, with no trace of irony, "that the light is always right in there. It's the benevolent glow of great wealth."

CHAPTER 14

We decided to stay on in Guadalajara for a few days. The opening of the Virgin of Guadalupe display had been delayed twenty-four hours for unexplained reasons. Naturally, in México, delays required no explanation. We also hadn't heard anything more from Botticelli. If it hadn't been for the $7,000 check in my wallet, the trip would have started to look like a bust, except to Maya. She'd gotten a boost from Almeida's attentions and gone off in a taxi downtown to a store she liked for lingerie. I didn't think the one had anything to do with the other; she'd planned that excursion before we left San Miguel. I didn't offer to drive her in that traffic, and she understood. I'd hidden the two new Matisses in our room, and Cody and I were hanging out in the dense garden of our B & B after she left. It was like a Noah's ark of vegetation, and it appeared that every known species of plant was represented. I hadn't seen jungle that thick since the Yucatan on our first case. What it lacked was any feeling of space and light. The shadowed gaps within the vines were crawling with shady life. I felt that vipers, ringed in lethal colors, pausing for a second or two to stare curiously at the tops of our heads, might be about to drop on us out of the treetops as we sat there. We kept tabs on the outside world through Maya's laptop. Somehow we still got a wi-fi signal through the wall-to-wall growth.

The rest of the place was like the garden, where collections of folk art crawled like a plague of jungle creatures over every wall. Masks, decorative plates, embroidered vests, paintings. The eye could not select a single object to focus on. All the vertical surfaces were *paved* with objects. You saw the entire field as a texture, but no single item within it. Clearly, for the owner, more was more. I thought it was less.

Yet our room was simply done, with only two pictures over the bed—bland lithographs of the same size, one of a woman crouching, the other of a peasant boy. They were OK, but one was in color and other in black and white.

We were just starting to consider whether it might soon be cocktail hour, when a new message popped up on the email screen. It came from Botticelli, via Gerson, and it was terse. Would we be able to show the two Matisses within the next hour in Tlaquepaque, a neighborhood of Guadalajara? And how odd was it that Botticelli would suggest Tlaquepaque in the next hour? But it was like Glass, so arrogantly to give us no warning, to keep us off balance. His self-importance hadn't diminished at all. Why would it? He was probably by now the greatest art thief in history who hadn't been backed by an army, as Napoleon, Stalin, and Goering had. Cody emailed back that we could, while I called the contact Delgado had given us in the Guadalajara Judicial Police. With any luck we'd have backup within moments, and the police could just haul the VRC director back to their dungeons to be held for Diego Delgado. I wasn't unhappy to have Maya remain clear of this confrontation—Glass had to be nursing a vendetta against her after the insulting way she'd gotten away from him with no help. Thinking back to his classroom manner, he hadn't ever taken women seriously as painters, and maybe not in any other way, although I was speculating there. Whenever a woman student with feminist instincts referred to women's historical role in painting, he would usually say, "Name one," holding up a single finger, although not his middle one.

"You don't think it's odd that Glass wants to meet us here in Tlaquepaque? We only mentioned Guadalajara to Botticelli, a much bigger playing field." Cody said this in a reflective tone as we cruised down Juarez in the direction of Niños Heroes. "It's almost as if he knows we're here. Do you think? How could that be? He must have spies."

"I know you're no fan of coincidence, but if he does know it, I can't think how he figured it out. He's smart in some ways, but not psychic, and positively stupid in others." Suddenly I thought of Sheila Roper. Where was she this afternoon? Knocking back a couple of margaritas, possibly, but was she following us as she promised on the night we met her? The thought was oddly comforting in a way I couldn't have explained. Maybe she could've read this situation better than we did. ESP would be helpful in this business. Maybe we could hire her as a consultant when we got back.

"It always makes me suspicious," Cody went on, "when coincidence appears to have a purpose. I don't know, I'm only thinking out loud here. Give me your take on it."

"For me, this connection has always been stretched thin, coming as it does through Gerson, and then to you. Now it's close and intimate. I feel like you do. There's something funny here. I don't know what."

"Hinky, I'd say." He folded his arms and scanned the street.

In a sprint we crossed the amateur speedway called Niños Heroes, where stopping, even for red lights, occurred only grudgingly by anyone driving. It was especially unconvincing to pedestrians trying to get to the other side. Beyond, the upscale areas of Tlaquepaque dissolved into a standard lower-class neighborhood, with dirty sidewalks and dreary colors. Trash whipped up in wind-blown spirals, before settling back in scattered piles. The paint colors were bargain table, and often changed in mid-wall. Whites were temporary. In most places, the most creative paint in view was the graffiti, which I reluctantly admitted could sometimes have great beauty, and usually a certain pizzazz, although I still didn't want to see it where it was. Here, people worked harder to survive, and 'middle class' was a term most would have had to look up, if they were literate and possessed a dictionary. Unfortunately, many people here can't read.

Two blocks in, we approached a rectangular athletic field—no more than the luxury of an open quarter of a block. The surface was gravel or sand. Two groups of kids were kicking soccer balls back and forth in the angular sunlight. Some of their tee shirts said, Bimbo, a big sponsor of local teams. It was not illicit fun; Bimbo made and sold bakery products all over México. But from the look of the area, that kind of fun may have been the best available, once it got dark and you could no longer see the balls.

This was the designated meeting place for the

exchange of my two faked masterpieces of stolen French art.

Cody and I both focused at the same time on the vehicle that had to be our contact: a white Suburban, immaculate. It waited beneath one of two meager trees that edged the playing field, the trunks painted white up to a meter above the soil line. No one moved along the street as we approached. The driver faced the sun, so he couldn't see us well as we moved toward him. Had he expected us to come up from behind? A miscalculation, because, now I could clearly see his face, as could Cody. It was a face we already knew.

"Bloody hell!" he said. "It's that short Armando guy from Almeida's place!"

"Look at the license plate. It's *Agave.* I remember it. I don't think he saw us, though."

So there it was. The vinegary taste of disappointment piling up behind my tongue was devastating. We'd been wrong, or I had, about the identity of the man behind the mask called Botticelli. I cruised on at the same speed with what I felt was a lot of poise going down to the end of the block, giving nothing way. It was like being on autopilot because I had no response for what had just happened. I could have been Morgan Freeman in *Driving Miss Daisy*, only less well paid, although I had the pace down perfectly. Rarely could I keep it together at that level of disappointment, but somehow I did.

"I'm wondering whether looking out the smoked glass side window of that Suburban just now was Vidal Almeida," I said. "That would cap this off nicely. He wouldn't have had the sun in his eyes at that angle."

Cody waved this away like a relative he didn't

want to see again. "He never came all the way down to the car entry. He doesn't know what you're driving."

"I don't know. All he needed was to be looking into the street just now, waiting for his picture seller to come. Anyway, we were dead wrong. I assumed Botticelli the collector was Glass, only because he liked girls in that strawberry blond style, and Botticelli the painter was also a connoisseur of the same look. But Almeida is a huge art collector too. He could just as easily have used the name for his own reasons. We completely misfired on this."

"I'm glad Maya wasn't here to see me blow this," Cody said, ruefully.

"She already knows you're human. I told her some time back."

"But we've never talked about it."

This made me smile. "Choose a better time to work it out. Some things are best left under the rug. Nonetheless, she's a Méxican woman. You'd like to believe Maya knows nothing about men. That way you can think she doesn't see the degree of your feeling for her, but that's the opposite of the truth. Women here know everything about men, Cody, even things you don't. *Especially* things you don't. Things you couldn't handle."

"You're saying they *can* handle them?" His slitted eyes looked at me from an angle beyond oblique.

"From long experience, starting in childhood. The relations are different here. Sex is always on the table, unless you're related by blood, and sometimes even then. I'll tell you about it later. Sometimes painters really do see things differently. So what do we do now, besides slink off into the underbrush?"

"I suppose there's no transaction anymore."

"There never was going to be a transaction. Now there's nothing at all. Ethically, how could I sell Almeida copied pictures? Think about it."

"Right, I forgot that part."

"I know what you're saying, but all the other faked pictures I sold him were sold *as* fakes. That's not how the Matisses were promoted. There can be ethics even in fakes."

"So you're saying we should just walk away from this. That's not your usual position."

"That's all we can do. Or should I stop and tell Almeida that yes, they're great but they're fakes and he can have them for $800? That Glass was present here was no more than our own fantasy—the game's over now. We can stay a couple of days longer until the Guadalupe picture goes up in the cathedral, take a look at it with Maya, speculate about what it *really* is, and then we go home and hang our new Matisses. I'll give you one. It's not a LeRoy Neiman, but what the hell. Neither am I."

"I suspect you wouldn't want to be on your best day."

"Thank you for seeing that."

"But he outsells you a thousand to one."

"I'm not everyone's cup of tea. I know that."

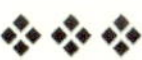

Maya was already back and seated in the garden when we returned. She stood up immediately, and putting her palms down, leaned across the table.

"Did Glass send you a message yet?"

"No. It's not Glass. Vidal Almeida is on the other end of this deal."

"What? He wants the Matisses? But I saw one of Glass's people that I recognized from the night they took the Bellas Artes show down. He was in *el centro* as I was coming back in the taxi. How could his boss not be here too?"

This was a shock, but I couldn't explain it. I gave her the story. When I finished, she pulled her ponytail tighter as if to focus her thoughts.

"Where was he?" said Cody, scratching his chin.

"Coming out of the underground parking garage alongside the cathedral plaza. The store I went to is on the same street three blocks down."

"He was on foot?"

"Right."

"So he had to be dropping off a vehicle in the garage," I said.

"That makes sense, but I didn't see him go in."

"This does not remotely compute," said Cody.

"It only doesn't compute because we started with the wrong set of assumptions," I said. "Forget Matisse, and forget Almeida. Look at this as new information, only that, almost like a new case. Glass's crew is here in Guadalajara, and he's not here for us, or our Matisses. You could be right—Glass, himself, may be here too. He's got another project of some kind going."

"A project near the cathedral," said Maya, folding her arms in the way she had when she was just tumbling to something. "There's only one thing going on at the cathedral that I know of that would interest him."

A brief silence followed as the same idea formed in a bubble over each of our heads.

"Do you think?" I said. "Would he really have the outrageous guts to do that?"

"You know his ego better than most," she said.

"But the Guadalupe picture isn't art, if that's what he's after," said Cody. "The man is an art thief."

"If it isn't art, then what else is it? Don't tell me it's a sixteenth century photo."

"More important," said Maya, "it hasn't been installed yet in the cathedral. Remember that unanticipated delay we heard about? Wouldn't that give Glass time to make a switch?"

CHAPTER 15
DR. BERNHARD GLASS

The director of the VRC stood looking out the long row of second-floor windows into the dark, narrow lane below. His hands were behind his back, alternately gripping and releasing each other as he rocked back and forth on his heels. This was more tension than he was used to, or cared to sustain. Droplets of sweat grew on his forehead; there had probably been no fresh air in this workroom for nobody knew how long. He had ordered no windows to be opened; he wanted nothing changed in the outer appearance of the place. His crew had watched the building for ten days after spotting its perfect hidden access, just eight blocks from the cathedral. No one had come or gone during that time.

It looked like the studio of a clothing designer, or custom maker. Perhaps theatrical costumes? Glass could only guess. Behind him were three rows of work tables, backed by mobile hanging racks, bins, boxes and bolts of fabric, trays of small parts like sequins and buttons, spools of thread. Coming in, he had counted four full-length mirrors on the walls. In this dim light, they reflected little more than his vague movements. Displayed on the table at his left were three dozen wigs. He could see that none of them were strawberry blond. From their disheveled look, they'd had a lot of use. It was 3:15 in the morning: zero hour for a plan five months in the making.

Glass heard a door latching softly from the van parked in the alley below. That was a mistake—he should be hearing nothing at all. Collin Welch moved swiftly from the rear of the van to the entry and out of his view—two seconds of exposure. He was carrying a large rectangular container no more than two inches thick.

"Here it is, Natty," said Glass. "To quote someone's commercial, it's the real thing."

"I'm eager to see it."

Glass caught a note in his voice that was something other than eagerness. Clearly, after copying it, Natty had his own views about the object. But the man was a painter, and painters were notorious for their deviant opinions. Look at that silly Paul Zacher. He had gotten lucky on a few guesses. It was no more than a shot in the dark, yet it had launched him on a voyage of subversion and interference. In light of all his carefully laid plans, Glass thought of it as chaos yapping at the gates of the VRC. Clearly, there could never be any substitute for true expertise, which included an appreciation for order, civility, and a decent respect for connoisseurship. A mere knack for smearing paint around on canvas didn't qualify. At least Natty was relatively docile and didn't mind his short leash.

Dr. Glass was not only a master of art history, but of strategy. In his view, this was what made him a perennial winner. The México City armored truck that delivered the Lady of Guadalupe picture to the Guadalajara cathedral at one A.M. had set off a chain of events months in the making. On Glass's outline, it was step #34. The

Guadalajara buyer had tipped Glass earlier on to the opportunity represented by the picture going on tour. At that point, it was in the advanced planning stages, but not yet public knowledge. But it was soon enough in the process for Glass to place one of his people as a security guard at the cathedral when the word went out that additional staff was needed. Influence matters in México, and timing matters anywhere.

Glass heard Welch on the stairs. This time, a little noise didn't matter. The man had come through.

At around one A.M. the *object*, as Glass thought of it, had been delivered to the cathedral and placed in the treasury. The archbishop had only appeared to unlock the ancient room for this important moment, then retired after relocking it, leaving security to the guard. He was not accustomed to being up at that time of night. The installation would take place the following day. The thick iron doors of the treasury had been locked with its ancient, massive key, and the rest of the cathedral entrances were secured in the normal way. The truck crew departed.

The windowless treasury room was located at the rear of the sacristy, an area off limits to the public. The security guard carried keys to the cathedral entrances and the sacristy, but not to the treasury. This key was kept in the private safe of the archbishop, within his bedroom next to the chancery. Two weeks earlier, in the middle of the night, the new security guard had admitted to the sacristy an expert on antique lock restoration supplied by Dr. Glass. Recognizing the lock as a type common in Spain in the second half of the seventeenth century, one he had restored and repaired a dozen versions of, the expert fashioned a new key for the treasury in less than an hour. It did not remotely resemble the original key, or any key at all, but it opened the lock even better.

It had worked equally well that night at 3:15, when Collin Welch and his crew were admitted to the sacristy by the security guard, where they removed the Virgin image and were gone again within four minutes. Welch remarked to the driver as they left that he'd never seen anything as low tech.

Since Natty had delivered the copy himself, Dr. Glass invited him to examine the original, something he'd never done before in all of their previous dealings. Naturally, Chiara was not included. She had stayed behind at the Villa del Ensueño, in the room they shared on the edge of Tlaquepaque. Natty imagined her pretending to be asleep while he dressed in the semi-darkness, padding around in his socks. When he slipped out the door with a tube under his arm, he knew she was lying awake wondering why the delivery had to be made in the middle of the night, and he'd been ready with a snappish response.

Natty's invitation was even more significant because Glass had only allowed the crew about thirty minutes to switch the images. Of course, Natty and the director had never been in the same town before at the time of delivery, either. It left Natty to think he might be made partner at some point, if this apparent increase in confidence continued. In the UK, that would be a natural progression for a key player in the company, one with his irreplaceable skills. He wasn't sure how well Glass understood this, and this wasn't the moment to bring it up. The director was bursting with triumph in a way Natty had never seen before. Clearly, Glass had more than money at stake in these ventures.

"A fabulous job, Natty. I usually get to see your version with the genuine article, but you never do, so it's not about confidence in your skills," said Dr. Glass. "It never was, in your case. When I first saw that small Renoir you did years ago, I knew a door was opening for both of us. I think I need a cognac. Pity there's nothing like that in this place. I should have brought some." An almost sentimental tone crept into his voice.

"I know. You sold that one right away. You said if I could do a Renoir, I could do anything." In fact, Natty did not believe this was true by a long shot. The kind of vague luminosity Renoir conveyed so well was not difficult to reproduce when you understood his brushwork. The French Academic painters, who were starting to lose favor in the same period as the Impressionists were gaining success, were much more difficult to duplicate. He sometimes wondered if Glass weren't full of pretentiousness in place of insight. He appeared to have little understanding of the painting process.

Working in the high-ceilinged, dusty room, Collin Welch had unscrewed the cover of the rosewood case and lifted the lid as they talked. He set a task lamp next to it.

Natty unrolled his own version of the Virgin and his eyes fastened on the two images resting on the worktable before them. He could easily tell them apart, yet the differences were miniscule. One concerned the color of the canvas. The piece he'd used, which one of Glass's people in México City had obtained from some old forgotten stock in a store room at the School of Fine Arts, was the slightest degree lighter in color. In the pigmented areas he thought of as caramel, his own were off just a hair. Had he put slightly too much burnt sienna in the mix? It must have been a fault of the print he worked from, because matching colors came to Natty as naturally as seeing. It was all in the eye.

Leaning over the original, he felt no awe, only interest in an object he believed had deceived generations of Méxicans from the most humble peasant to the sharpest of scholars. Where was its power? In quality, it was not a remarkable painting. He didn't feel it was even an average piece, for the period. With no special identification, people would hardly pause to look at it grouped with other pictures. It looked like just one more routine devotional from a small town where the nearest art school was far away. He knew better than to ask Glass what he was going to get for it.

Natty understood what made this piece so special—a simple, yet critical element. As Bernard Berenson, the great, and occasionally corruptible, art expert, had once said of a mediocre Renaissance painting, "Change that frame and you'll make it a masterpiece." The Virgin of Guadalupe image was totally about the frame, although it didn't possess one in conventional terms. The "frame" in this case was the dense aura of myth and tradition developed and promoted by the Church, accumulated layer by layer over centuries like the smoky residue of incense thickening on the piers of a cathedral.

This had little to do with the almost pitiful relic he was now looking at inside the fine wooden case. Natty bent closely over the face, from the corner of his eye sensing Glass's hand almost lifting in alarm to stop him from touching it. Always the curator, he thought. Inches away, the pinched features faced him coldly. That it was paint, rather than some heavenly pigment, was clear. Natty looked deeply into the lady's eyes, searching for any trace of the thirteen miraculous figures of legend, curving to match their contour. It was the ultimate religious article of the Americas, yet her pupils were as blank and empty as outer space. In his own version, Natty had wanted to add a pinpoint of reflected light.

Glass drew him back by the elbow, and two of his crew switched the images with gloved hands as they walked away. Natty's copy, with its new layers of archival cushioning, was sealed into the rosewood container. The genuine image was enclosed in a less distinguished steel box.

"Amen," said Dr. Glass, with a chuckle. "You'll find an extra thousand pounds on your paycheck this month."

How many pieces of silver would that be, Natty thought, at the current rate of exchange? Just about thirty? After all, these were British pounds sterling, weren't they?

CHAPTER 16

My cell phone rang at three o'clock that morning. This is the principal risk of having one if you forget to switch it off. Although I was able to put my hand on it by the third ring after slapping the night stand a few times, I was too vague at that moment to ask myself whether or not I wanted to answer it.

"Zacher."

"I'm really sorry to wake you up, Paul. It's Sheila Roper. Do you remember our conversation?"

I yawned profusely and rubbed my eyes with my left hand. "Of course. I suppose you're suddenly seeing everything again now. Can you also see that I'm naked?"

Something like the sound of blushing followed. Hot blood, I thought, in a confined space.

"No, I can never see what I want to see most."

"That was quick. Quicker than I am, at the moment. What's going on, Sheila?"

"I'm with Chiara."

"OK, great job. I'm glad you called me at this ungodly hour, but who's Chiara?"

"She's Natty Bollander's girlfriend."

"Of course." I struggled to plug this in for a moment, but it was like I was having a power outage, not uncommon in México, in my mind. It meant that nothing would compute. "Are we talking about the same case here, Sheila, because this doesn't mean anything to me so far, but keep going. Or is this all about a case that hasn't come in yet? I acknowledge that you've been ahead of me before."

Maya had awakened and was following this with interest, leaning on one elbow and facing me. I switched on the lamp at the nightstand.

"Natty Bollander made a flawless copy of the Virgin of Guadalupe," said Sheila. "Chiara told me he's out delivering it tonight."

"He's delivering the Virgin of Guadalupe tonight." I repeated this for Maya's benefit.

She leaped out of bed and began pulling on her clothes, then ran outside and up the stairs to Cody's room.

"Tell me the story," I said, "all of it." I got up and started dressing, holding the phone to my head with my shoulder as I hopped around pulling on my pants and socks.

The story was pure Sheila Roper. An image had flashed into her mind yesterday of a barrel-chested man comparing two copies of the Virgin of Guadalupe, both taped upside down on a wall. He was going over them point by point. Sheila didn't know what this meant, except that it was connected to Maya's kidnapping, although she wasn't sure how or why. Her system lacked any connections between the images. The only other conversation we'd had with her was when Maya called her after our return from Texas, thanking her for her input. Sheila repeated her intention of keeping us informed of any further insights she might have. Privately, I thought we wouldn't hear from her again. How many future insights could there be, when they were on some kind of automatic pilot that no one understood, least of all, Sheila Roper herself?

After the two images, she'd seen nothing more, other than a hotel façade. With a growing sense of urgency, she found the hotel on the Internet, with an address in Guadalajara. When she saw this, she'd had a sudden feeling Maya was there too, in a room with the walls covered by ugly masks. Had she been kidnapped again? Sheila spent several hours trying to resist the impulse to go there, even going to bed at one point. But sleepless at 10:30, when she had another flash of an armored car approaching Guadalajara, she threw some things in an overnight bag and got in her car. She felt at that point more would be coming to her once she was on the road.

"With your skills, I don't suppose you ever need GPS," I said. It's the only way to find your way around México, where the signage on the roads is laughable.

"When I got to the hotel I described the barrel-chested guy to the desk clerk. He sent me up to their room and Chiara answered the door. She was already awake, and, being Italian, once I introduced myself, she didn't find it strange that I'd seen all of that. She said that her friend Natty was out delivering the version he'd painted, and she was eager to fill in the blanks."

"So the two of you are going after him? Why is she part of this? You'd think she'd want to protect him. Where's her loyalty?"

"I'll let her tell you. We're parked now in front of your bed and breakfast."

I hadn't told her where we were staying. Cody and Maya walked in the door at this point.

"I guess you turned up a lead," he said.

"Let's go. They're already waiting out front." I could see he had his gun in his belt under a voluminous shirt that still showed the creases of being folded in his suitcase. Maya and I both pulled ours out, and we left.

At that point it was about 3:20, a period of brief and refreshing respite between the chaos of late night traffic and the turbulence of morning rush hour. We waited at the curb as Chiara stepped out of the car, a tall, attractive Italian woman with full, expressive lips and a slender, but still sensuous, build. Her gaze was frank and conveyed the sense of someone coming out of a dream or illusion, and wanting to establish the facts up front with people she was meeting for the first time. It might even have been a way to test them out for herself. As an investigator, I welcomed this, especially at that hour of the night, when I was about three and a half cups of strong coffee away from full strength. Normal coherence developed about halfway through the second. After a round of introductions, Maya spoke first, to Sheila. She was all business.

"We're ready to take this to the next level. What do you see now?"

"Nothing." A small shrug.

Cody sighed, painfully. He could have still been sleeping.

"What?" Sheila said, both palms turned upward. "I can't do it on command. I said that before."

"It's just that I'd like to be able to gather information in a normal way," he said. "That's how I was trained. No offense, but I'm out to sea here."

"So go ahead and gather," Sheila said, pulling a silk scarf closer around her neck. I realized she'd been driving for four hours, and she was a little edgy.

"Listen," I said. I wanted to pull this together because it felt like it was going off the rails. After all, as the former head of the agency, I had once occupied a position of trust. "Point one. Where do you think Natty is now?"

"I can see him! Wow! You asked me something, and I got it right away! He's in a poorly lit place full of costumes and disguises. Wigs, even. He's standing next to a dress model with another man. I can't see his face. I didn't even have to hold your hand to get that! You're good, Paul."

Chiara gave Sheila a strange look.

Maya gave me a dig in the ribs, invisible to the rest, I'm sure. She knew I was occasionally good, but she got snorky when I was good with anyone else. Not that she knew exactly what good meant in this case. I didn't either.

She said a few words to Chiara, and with a gesture to me that said, stay here, she and the Italian woman walked inside the bed and breakfast.

"Is it a dress designer studio?" said Cody.

"It could be. But it's so dark, it's hard to tell."

"Where did the armored car go?" I said.

Sheila shook her head. "Don't know. I felt it was headed somewhere in Guadalajara. It was no more than a glimpse."

"You didn't get any sense of what was inside?"

"No. I thought it was odd that they were traveling at night. I'm not sure why. I suppose they have to when they're transporting valuables over a long distance."

"You didn't see the license plate," I said.

"No."

I wondered if it had been from México City.

CHAPTER 17
MAYA SANCHEZ

Maya guided Chiara back through what looked like the movie set for *The African Queen*. Ground lights showed the paths. They found a small cast-iron table at the back near her room and lit a candle. Chiara ignited a cigarette from the candle.

"I know how it is to be with an artist," Maya said. "Paul's been painting for more than twenty years. I've posed for him almost forty times." Chiara gave her a bleak smile, as if she were missing the point.

"But does Paul do copies? I think not." Chiara's English was heavily accented with Italian, and her tone suggested a difference in kind between Paul and Natty.

"He does, even though it's not his favorite kind of work. We came here to deliver three devotional pictures to a private collector. But most of the time, maybe 95% of the time, he's doing his own work. Paul is always full of ideas."

"So I think that's the problem. Copies are the only things Natty does. He's very talented, and I know he could be doing his own work too, but it never happens. He's afraid of something." In the dense foliage above, a large bird fluttered and thrashed about for a moment before settling down again. Slivers of bark dropped to the table between them.

"What would he be afraid of?" asked Maya. Paul tackled ambitious projects all the time, and if they ever scared him, he didn't show it.

"Failure, I think. I don't know what else." She blew a long plume of smoke into the trees. "He never talks about his art and he doesn't try to find a gallery. It's different from your husband."

"Paul's not my husband."

"He doesn't want to marry you?" A look of surprise came over her face.

"He asked me a while back in Oaxaca, and I said he had to ask my father on his knees. That was a mistake."

"He's too proud?"

"No, we haven't been back to México City. That's where my father lives."

"You should go there now. I gave up waiting. Now I'm giving up on the whole thing. I've only been fooling myself. In my dream, even though I worked in an insurance office, I was married to an important painter. We had friends who were cultured and intelligent, always in good clothes. We went to Natty's gallery shows on opening night in Paris and New York and drank champagne. Even though it was serious, we were always laughing, always happy. Afterward, we gathered with friends and celebrated late into the night." An ugly curl formed on Chiara's lips.

"You're very angry."

Chiara nodded slowly. "I am angry from being stupid, that's all. It was my mistake from the beginning. I made him into what I wanted him to be, but it was only in my head. Now they're going to steal the Virgin of

Guadalupe."

"Did he say that?"

"No, Natty would never tell me what he was doing. But what else can it be? What other reason would he have to deliver the copy of it in the middle of the night? I bet my life on a criminal."

Looking into Chiara's face, Maya was silent for a moment before she went on. "And he makes money doing this copy work?"

"The museums in Florence pay him for each piece he restores, but he has a regular deposit from a company called Glassworks Party, Ltd. that's much larger. Thousands of pounds every month. I looked at the records on his laptop."

"Glassworks. I see." Maya was nodding as lines were converging inside her head. Glassworks was a perfect name for the director's shady enterprises, as if they were all transparent. A nervous twittering resumed in the foliage around them. Maya felt they were intruding on the local fauna at that hour.

"I thought it might be for stained glass designs, although I haven't seen him doing any, and for making so much money, I would have seen something of them. Have you heard of that company?"

"I might have, if the owner is Dr. Bernhard Glass."

"Natty mentioned a Dr. Glass! He said he makes copies for him to show how counterfeit pictures might be done. I haven't met him."

"We might meet him soon. I've seen one of his people here, and I've met him before. He had me kidnapped last month."

"What! He is that kind of man?"

"Worse. He ordered a murder in my town, San Miguel de Allende."

"Do you know this?"

"It's clear enough. What would you like to happen here?"

"I'd like Natty to end his part in this. How dangerous is it?"

"People could die. More than one, even."

"Your agency has killed people in the past? Sheila told me you were detectives."

"I've killed two myself. I'm not proud of it, but sometimes you have no choice. Dr. Glass wouldn't hesitate to kill any of us, I think. Especially me."

Chiara leaned back in her chair and folded her arms. "I was angry before, Maya, but now you're saying Natty has led me into this, even when he knew what it all meant? I have a good life insurance, subsidized by my company, but he's the beneficiary. With a lot of money after I was dead, would he then paint real pictures, his own true life's work? I don't think so. Am I going to give him the opportunity to go on as he has been? It's too late to change my beneficiary, from here. You can't do it online. When I get back home I'll make it my sister."

Maya's arm came up slowly and swept these thoughts from the table. They belonged more in that summing up phase that occasionally happened at Harry's on Hidalgo, when each of the agency members got to second-guess their own performance, while no one else said a word. It was a unique kind of performance review, but it worked.

"You're not going to die, Chiara. Maybe no one

dies this time, aside from that thief of Glass's that he ordered killed early on. That and getting paid are always my hope, anyway. Of course, sometimes both get away from me. I'm the head of the Zacher Agency, but I've come to realize how little that means in controlling events."

"You know what I feel? I'll tell you." Chiara leaned across the table and thrust out her chin. "That Natty's been unfaithful to me. It's like he's been screwing my sister, or worse, my *mother.*" Chiara leaned to the side and, with extreme contempt, spat into the bromeliads.

"OK, then," said Maya, in an even more conciliatory tone, "I think we can still work together on this, now that you've gotten that out in the open. Although I think Natty's infidelity may have been more an offense against your idea of what he was. What we have now is unity of purpose. My plan is that you don't die; none of us does, and we recover the Virgin of Guadalupe. Your company keeps its insurance settlement, OK? Then, without Natty, you live on to find a real painter, producing his own stunning work, and have champagne toasts from Prague to Paris, during your children's school holidays, of course."

"I like that! Are you part Italian?"

"No, but I'm all woman. It's easy to see what *you* want when it's almost exactly what I want too."

Chiara stubbed out her cigarette in the onyx ashtray and stood up. At that moment her cell phone rang.

CHAPTER 18

Maya and Chiara came out to the sidewalk. Chiara was on her cell phone. She moved off a few paces down the street. I could hear her voice rising in both pitch and volume. I moved closer to Maya's ear.

"What did she say?"

"She's ready to help us, but she doesn't know much. Her boyfriend, Natty Bollander, is working for Glass and he painted a copy of the Virgin. She says that all he does is copies."

"Bingo," I said. "Then they're doing the switch now. The armored car must have been bringing the original to the cathedral. That's why Sheila saw it."

"They'll wait until it's inside the cathedral and the armored car is gone," said Cody. "Those security guys are armed to the teeth."

"Are you getting anything now?" I asked Sheila.

"Nothing."

I was dying to hear Chiara's phone conversation, but she was too far away to make out more than the tone of it. Finally I heard her snap the cover shut and she walked back toward us. We were all looking at her expectantly. She shrugged.

"Natty's back at the hotel. He didn't seem

surprised that I wasn't there. I told him I wasn't coming back. I'd had enough. I wasn't going to go to prison for being his accomplice."

"What did he say?" asked Maya.

Chiara's face took on a grim look. "He said I could do whatever the hell I wanted."

"But is that what you wanted?"

"I wanted Natty to beg me to stay with him. I wanted him to say he'd give it up for me."

Sheila Roper moved over and put an arm around her. "He's deeply regretting it now," she said.

"You can see that?" Under the streetlight, her eyebrows went up and her eyes took on a glimmer of hope.

"No, but I know it must be true. You can trust these insights."

"Where are you staying?" asked Cody.

"At the Villa del Ensueño. It's…"

"I know where it is," I said. "Cody and I are going to pay a visit to Natty."

No one protested. They weren't needed for this and I didn't want Chiara to see us apply a little muscle to Natty if we had to. I also didn't know whether he might be armed without Chiara knowing it. We got into the van once the women were back inside the bed and breakfast.

"This is our only shot unless Sheila has another breakthrough," Cody said. "And her insights seem to be focused mainly on detail, rather than the larger sense of what's going on. She sees the locations more easily than the ideas."

"Better than seeing nothing, which is where we were before she arrived."

"I'm not saying that. She's a godsend." He eased

his pistol out of his belt and checked the cylinder.

I drove through the empty streets toward the northern edge of Tlaquepaque, where it began to merge into Guadalajara. The hotel was barely more than two kilometers away. The town was eerily silent after the nonstop rush hour of the day and evening. I felt like the silence set the mood for some violent confrontation ahead, not with Natty, but with the big people on the other end of the action, if we could connect with them. I had the sudden thought that I should try to reach the cop whose number Delgado had given us, but it was late in the night, and we had no assurance that we'd ever encounter Glass. My sense was that he preferred to stay buried behind multiple layers of his people during a move like this.

We parked down the street a hundred yards from the Villa del Ensueño. No one was moving in either direction. The façade formed a shallow inward curve that provided for a covered drive large enough to accommodate a single car, loading or unloading. It was no surprise that the door was locked at that hour. Cody rang the bell. On the back of his belt I saw the shape of his handcuffs. I knew he had his gun in front under his shirt, and usually he carried a small flashlight with his lock picks. This was his standard working kit.

After a long moment, a woman's voice responded.

In English, I said we'd like to see Natty Bollander. After a pause, the door was opened by a Méxican woman.

"He is expecting you?"

"I'm his brother from Chicago," said Cody, with a broad, but apologetic, grin.

"He has room number two, at the top of the stairs

on the left." She gestured to a staircase at the right of the reception desk.

The second floor had only two rooms in this part of the building, so Natty was not hard to find. Cody knocked softly on the door. Natty answered immediately, but without opening it. "Chiara?"

"It's about Chiara," I said. "We need to talk." As I heard the bolt slide open, I looked at Cody. He was ready for anything. His left hand was on his gun and his right rested on the door eight inches above the knob. When it opened about four inches on the chain, part of a face looked out at us. The face saw two men and Natty tried to slam the door shut again. Cody's hand held it open, and slowly forced it to the limit of the chain, where, with a deft move of his wrist, he snapped the chain mounting free of the jamb without much noise, and pushed the door open all the way. I closed it behind us. Natty stood there nervously watching us.

"I guess you don't have a gun." Cody said. "I do. So in case you're just being cool and waiting for a good opportunity to make a move, there isn't going to be one." He pulled his shirt aside to show Natty the butt of his pistol. So did I. "Whatever you do, I'll be faster than you. Have a seat."

With a firm and sour set to his lips, Natty sat on a loveseat next to the closet, and Cody pulled up a chair from the desk to face him. I stayed on my feet and looked around, watching him narrowly at the same time in case he decided to do something rash. If Cody killed him, we wouldn't get much out of him. I never depend on deathbed confessions. The room wasn't bad. The furniture was the leather and slat *equipal* design that the locals in

Tlaquepaque did very well. High end folk furniture, as I thought of it. When Natty volunteered nothing, Cody started out on him.

"We met your girlfriend tonight. I liked her right away, and she had an interesting tale to tell. I bet you can imagine. What surprised me was that she was so disappointed in you, because she also felt you were a first class painter."

"Or could be, if you used your own ideas," I added over my shoulder. I suddenly felt like we were bullies. It's one of those job skills you need to have in this business.

"Paul here would know. He's quite the painter himself. Chiara didn't say how long you two had been together, only that it was over, and it seemed like she was kind of bitter. Don't know the Italians very well, but when women start spitting when they say your name, I guess they've had about enough." Maya had told us this while Chiara was off on her phone.

"She doesn't know a bloody thing about it," said Natty. "If she told you things about me, she was making them up. That girl's got a big imagination."

"Quite a bit bigger than yours, I think." I looked at him straight on for the first time. "Isn't that the problem, Natty? Although you can paint anything, you can't think of what to paint on your own. I saw that a few times in art school. People like you were called 'mechanics.' While it suggests a strong technical ability, it was still not a flattering term, because those people had no soul. That's an even bigger issue, and harder to fix."

Natty looked back at me with a kind of startled hatred, like he'd been read right through his innermost being by a casual stranger walking past him.

"Who are you?" His British accent made this sound even more indignant than it would have in American English.

"Just another painter. I've done the occasional copy too, although Dr. Bernhard Glass doesn't have me on his payroll. Maybe he'll call me after you've gone to prison. You see, when I do a copy, I always sign my own name on the back. I'll bet when we look at the back of the Virgin of Guadalupe picture, we won't find yours. What *will* we find there, Natty? It's time you started talking. Glass isn't going to want to take the rap for this, and here's your chance to get out in front of him before it all comes down. Whose side do you want to be on when that happens?"

Natty appeared to retreat into himself. How had we gotten all this information? I was almost surprised myself at the way it had come together. If I hadn't been a painter myself, I wouldn't have known what I was looking at. Chiara's insights had tipped it, and Sheila's had almost wrapped it up.

The silence dragged on for about five minutes. It felt like twenty to me, and how long it felt to Natty, I couldn't imagine. Cody and I were both good at waiting. At the right moment, Cody said, "Of course there is still a way out, here. That's the good thing. The main task in a situation like this is not to hang someone, even though they might be guilty as hell. It's getting the stolen goods back. You probably noticed that Paul and I are not the police. That's where you got lucky tonight."

Cody was nodding in an encouraging way toward the end of this statement. His job—he often saw himself as more a negotiator than a prosecutor, although it always started out as investigator—was to cancel the effect of the crime. With no one dead, that was still doable at this point.

"If you ask my advice," I said, "when you catch a break like this, Natty, you jump all over it. The breaks have already started to fade away for you. It began with Chiara splitting with all that stuff she downloaded to disc about Glassworks Pty. from your laptop. We haven't have time to go through all of it yet, but the financial records we saw were enough to tell the story."

This was a stretch, but not much of one. Natty raised his palms toward us as if holding us at bay.

"I swear I didn't know what Glass was doing. He told me he was using my copies in his lectures about fakes. After all, he ran the VRC, didn't he? It was all about fakes. He never dealt with a genuine picture in his life, once he became director. How could I know?" After his stolid manner, his gestures became dramatic, as if trying out for the role of a lifetime.

"And it was quite natural that you would deliver those copies to him in the middle of the night," said Cody, leaning closer into Natty's face. "They must fade easily in the sun, was that it?"

He swallowed hard, and a tiny rivulet of drool descended from the left corner of his mouth. Some people became dry in the mouth during a crisis, but apparently some other people didn't. I suddenly felt like I was looking at Nixon. Natty was taking no responsibility for what he'd done.

When he had no response to this, Cody let another silence develop.

"I'm going to put an offer on the table," Cody

said, after a cluster of long moments. "It's the only one I have. Like you, I don't possess a grand imagination, and the only thing I can think of if you don't accept, is that we turn this over to the authorities. We have friends in the judicial police in San Miguel. One I'm thinking of in particular. Why, his career would be made if he recovered the stolen image of the Virgin of Guadalupe. He'd be a national hero. Imagine! The greatest religious artifact of the Americas! You'd need the National Guard to protect you from being ripped limb from limb by the mob. And just imagine your treatment in a México prison!"

Natty leaped up and put his hands out in front of him.

"OK. OK, where do I sign? What do you want?"

I stepped forward and leaned into his face from about six inches away. "We want it back, intact, Natty. Nothing less. Plus whatever you've got that will put Glass away for good. Now, where is the Virgin of Guadalupe?"

CHAPTER 19

Private Detective is not the next rank above Eagle Scout. Its standards are more flexible. You don't have to read a suspect his rights, and you can lie about anything in trying to beat the truth out of him. It's not likely to be admissible in court because you're not ever going to court. I even felt pretty good about the way we'd handled Natty. It was no longer an investigation; it was more like a pounding. Sometimes you just have to roll up your sleeves and go for it.

All the same, I did feel a minor twinge of sympathy for Natty because he was a painter. I imagined that his inability to be creative must be like a talented writer with a block. You knew you could do it, if you could only get started. The first word was the hardest one to find. I suspected he might not be sufficiently lost in his work. The ego has to be jettisoned; there's no room for it on the canvas. As people often say: it's not about you.

Natty had laid out the whole program for us, even producing a list of all the paintings he'd copied for Glass. He had printed a paper copy of it as if to remind himself what a great painter he was—all those masterpieces coming from his hand! That paper could become a blueprint for recovery for all the museums and private collectors involved. Did he ever know where the genuine paintings went? Not really. Dr. Glass liked to hint when the collector was an important man, but he had never said any names outright.

"Didn't he even give you a hint this time?" said Cody. Something in his voice suggested the importance of the question.

"In a way. He called him Señor Tequila." He shrugged. "That could be anyone around here, I guess. He wasn't giving anything away." His tone was ingratiating now.

In the silence that followed, neither Cody nor I gave anything away, either. We left with the list and some other records. They included Natty's contact information, but I wasn't thinking much about him anymore. The police could catch up with him and train him as their insider witness. Natty acknowledged that Glass was in town, but said he didn't know how to reach him. Privately, I didn't buy this. The director must have phoned Natty and left his number on Natty's cell phone, but I no longer cared. I thought about taking it from him so we could get Glass's number, but if he called him we couldn't talk without tipping him off, so I didn't. I did take the cardboard tube from what I assumed was the reproduction he worked from. I could anticipate a potential use for it once we connected with the original Virgin picture. Only later did I notice it was addressed to Glassworks Pty., C/O N. Bollander, General Delivery, *Entrega General*, Colonia Polanco, D. F., México.

I was thinking more about Vidal Almeida, Señor Tequila. Who else could it be? There might be other collectors among the tequila distillers, but then why deliver the Virgin to someone in Tlaquepaque? Natty had told us that when he left the dressmaking studio, Collin Welch was taking both images away. There was no point in our trying to find it. Glass would be long gone and Welch would be placing Natty's version in the cathedral treasury, then delivering the original to the client.

"No doubt who we're up against, is there?" said Cody as I drove back to the hotel.

"I don't see who else it could be."

"We could call in the police, tell them Almeida's got the Virgin."

"I'm sure he owns the police," I said, "and if asked, the cathedral will say they've still got the Virgin in their treasury. Who's going to contradict them? They don't want to look like they've bungled it. It'll be their biggest money-maker in decades."

"I don't like the other choices."

"There's only one."

"That's what I don't like."

"I think we don't care about Natty's copy at this point," I said. "We won't need it until we get the original back. If we *can* get it back."

"And what exactly is the original in your view? We should all understand this, and you're the expert." I could feel his eyes boring into the side of my head.

"I think the image is a routine devotional picture that's been sanctified by Church promotion for several hundred years. It was painted by conventional means on linen, because otherwise it wouldn't have lasted this long. From its appearance, it's a modest relic of its kind, sanctified by many generations of intense hype."

A moment of silence followed while I parked near our bed and breakfast. I looked at Cody, expecting more. I wasn't wrong.

"Then why, in God's name, are we going to switch them back? What does it matter? You want to take this battle right into their trenches. Aren't they playing the fool for going to all this trouble over—not exactly nothing—but damn close to it?"

A sharp rap on my window pulled me out of this. I didn't have a good answer anyway. I could have said that, like a lot of things, it was mostly about what people thought more than about reality. But why did I think that was reasonable? It was more just an instinct than a good reason for doing something so dangerous. I realized that Maya was standing there waiting. Cody got out and opened the rear door for her. I brought her up to date on our conversation with Natty Bollander.

"I've got my gun," she said. "Let's go, then, if you're ready. Sheila and Chiara are planning their own move."

"At least they've got a guide," said Cody, "in an on and off sort of way."

"There's some disagreement about whether it's worth it." I brought Maya up to speed on our present discussion. "Cody doesn't think we should do the Church a favor and return the Virgin to them."

A mild snort came from the back seat. "I don't think the Catholic Church has ever done a favor for this country that it didn't collect for ten times over," said Maya, her arms folded and her shoulders thrown back. "Anyway, as you've apparently pointed out, the Virgin of Guadalupe picture was always a fake in terms of its origins, and was cynically set up for veneration by the Church. They gave all us needy Méxicans our own homegrown relic to be proud of. They wanted us to have a pilgrimage site like the ones in Europe to support their local episcopal palaces."

This argument didn't surprise me. According to what she'd told me several times in the past, her family had always been anticlerical. They had taken sides against the Church during the Cristero War in the twenties, and probably even before that. It could have gone as far back as President Juarez in the 1860s, when he stripped the Church of all its property except the church buildings themselves. She'd reminded me that from the Conquest until then, the clergy had always been the largest landowners in México. It was land that belonged to the Indians, whose title had never been considered.

I looked at my watch. It was too late now to catch anyone delivering the Virgin to Almeida's mansion. Thinking of the last time we'd taken on Glass's crew, it wouldn't have been a good idea anyway.

"So what do we do, then?" said Cody.

"Am I the ethics guru now?" I said. "Painters don't know much about ethics, except in the studio. I think, though, that in terms of the people who believe in it, and they're still here by the tens of millions, it would definitely be meaningful to them to have the original, no matter what it really is. I'm not going to tell them what they can believe in, whether I agree with them or not. If the Church is telling them what to think, so be it—that's what they feel is their job. The world is full of institutions telling people what to believe. You make your choice, and by doing that, you point your life in one direction or another. Each of us has done that. It happened to you, Maya, when you grew up in a family of unbelievers. You must have chosen to follow that or reject it and go back to the Church."

"So you're comfortable with that?" she said. "Allowing people to go on believing a lie or a legend? What about being enlightened? Doesn't that matter? I thought this was a new century."

"Everybody already thinks they're enlightened, so why not be comfortable with it? What's nonsense to us is real to them. We don't all have to think alike, and no one has a monopoly on the truth. How many people believe what I believe? A lot of people would consider it nonsense. I'd be the first to admit that."

Silence. After a while Cody said, "But you're a painter. You couldn't expect anybody to think like you do. You see painters as a threat to the public order. You've said yourself a number of times that they generate chaos."

"Well, I've never been a missionary," I said, "and I'm not going to start now. I'm happy thinking the way I do even if that means I'm a minority of one. Here's the most important aspect of this to me—it offends me that this issue is being decided by a *thief*, and that's where it rests right now. I think we should return the original 400 year-old fake virgin icon to the Church and walk away. That's the Boy Scout solution, just as you said earlier, Maya. We will have done our good deed. Of course, that does mean we'll have to steal it back and switch it with the other one—a mere detail."

"And, if we do it right, and survive, no one will know that we did it," said Maya, "so what is the point? Everyone concerned will still be fooled just as they were before we got into this."

I sat there for a while trying to assemble the next

rung of this argument, but I wasn't getting anywhere.

"The three of us will know it," said Cody, quietly. "Sometimes ethics means no more than that. Maybe that's even the *soul* of ethics, when you do the right thing and no one else knows it. No one puts your name in the paper. I'm starting to think Paul's right, and it even sounds like something *I* would have said. There's no perfect solution to this, but that particular one is better than walking away, knowing the kind of injustice that was done. Knowing that Glass won again! Sometimes that's as close as you can get. Right now Vidal Almeida is laughing at the millions of people who're venerating a fake picture, and he thinks he has the real one. Just how superior do you have to be? That makes me more than uncomfortable, and it's not because I'm a believer, because I'm not. My ethics come from somewhere else."

"Of course, he's venerating a fake picture too," said Maya, "in terms of its real origins. He's no smarter than they are. We can be laughing at him as we all walk away from this upright. We weren't taken in by anybody, even our own need to believe."

"So are we the smartest ones then?" I was recalling my earlier musings about how smart our opponents had been over all our cases.

"We won't know that part until this is over," said Cody, "but I know what my bet is. We're going to prove it or not in a big way."

Of course, how smart we really were was going to be established more definitively in short order. We outvoted Maya two to one to go for it. I pulled away from the curb and headed toward Niños Heroes, where I took a right. I was in no hurry, and that time of night, you can actually drive as if you weren't. I had no idea what we were going to do. I found myself thinking about Maya and her stolen switchblade in Texas. I saw it against Glass's bulging neck in the scene she'd described in his office. It was a comforting image. We were all good improvisers when the situation called for it. This one was yelling for those skills.

We came at Independencia from the bottom of the street. I parked the van around the corner out of sight. Glass's crew had seen it during Maya's kidnapping, and Almeida's people and his security system knew it from our visit. God knows what else that system knew. I didn't want to think about it. We walked a short way in, where we came even with a life-size bronze sculpture group of the founding fathers of México. Frozen in time, they were advancing up the street. Here was Ignácio Allende, the hero of our town, and the subject of Maya's biography of his early years. The Aldama brothers, also of San Miguel. La Corregidora of Querétaro, Father Morelos, and Father Hidalgo, whose mouth, open as if to give the cry of independence and liberty as in 1810, was stuffed with a baby's pacifier, in latex, not bronze. Méxicans love a good joke, and I didn't care to pause to speculate on the meaning of this. Had he been silenced by subsequent developments? We scattered motionless within the cluster of statues as we surveyed the scene.

While Almeida's mansion was the grandest mansion on the street, it was not the only one. We faced a string of them on both sides. Next to his, toward us, taller but more modest, stood a white stucco house of substantial size. It was plainer in decoration and style. No lights were lit in the upper windows, but that was also true of every other building we could see. My watch said 4:30.

"I don't think we want to take a run at Almeida's place directly," said Cody. "We know he's got armed security and they're probably on special alert because of the Virgin's arrival. We'd never get in."

"The neighboring place is taller," I said. "If we can get in there, we might be able to drop into Almeida's from the common wall. It would be good to know first if anyone's home."

"We can just ring the bell," said Maya. "I'll do it. You guys wait here." Once she realized she'd been outvoted, she was in all the way. That's how Maya was; she never held back.

She walked directly up to the white mansion and pressed the bell. Even if no one came down to answer, at least a light might go on above and we would instantly be gone. That would tell us what we wanted to know, and we could move around the corner and see what the building next to Almeida's place on the Cruz Verde side looked like. We waited among the sculptures as she rang again.

When there was no response to the third ring, Maya stepped away from the door and gestured to us.

"I don't think it really rang inside. I didn't hear anything," she said as we came up.

This close, I noticed a set of four screw holes in the façade at eye level on each side of the entry, as if a pair of bronze plaques about two feet by three had once been mounted there.

"I wonder if it was a business at one time," said Cody.

It would not be unusual in México, where urban zoning is often nonexistent, or at best sketchy, to have a mansion converted into a business or consulate next to a property like Almeida's. They still would have façade design controls in a neighborhood like this, but what you did inside your property would be less a concern. I could easily imagine a pair of cast bronze signs flanking the door. They would be the only visible change from residence to business on a property that had once housed a wealthy family.

Cody scanned the latch and dead bolt for a moment. After looking up and down the street, he pulled out his lock picking kit and made a selection while I shone his penlight on the leather case. I checked my watch. Maya and I sat down on a nearby bench, shoulder to shoulder, like young lovers. Cody was more hidden in the deeper shadows behind us. It took him nine minutes.

"I think we're in good shape," he said, taking a step back. "This place isn't used much, or if it is, they're not coming and going through this entry, judging from how stiff the lock was. Maybe the house is empty." He pushed the door open. Crossing the vestibule inside, we climbed five steps. The only available light was from the moon, entering in long, dusty shafts from a glass covering high over the central courtyard ahead. On the arch at the top of the steps Cody shone his penlight on a trio of faces and shoulders in bas relief. They were all singing. It looked like an operatic trio.

"This must be *The Opera*!" I said softly. "It's a famous restaurant from years ago. I never knew where it was, other than that it had been a fixture in Tlaquepaque. It was a place where you could see Pavarotti or Callas dining after the performance, or Placido Domingo." It had been a Mecca for traveling companies playing the Guadalajara Opera after their first run in México City.

"I think I've heard of it," Maya said. She touched the wall with her fingertips, and then rubbed them together. "It's been closed for a long time, judging from the dust."

On all sides, an arcaded loggia surrounded the courtyard on both floors. The center was filled with tables, with the accompanying chairs set upside down around the rim. I couldn't see the floor clearly in the dim light, but I could smell the dust in the air as we moved along kicking it up. We must have been leaving a trail.

"This is just what we want," said Cody in a normal tone. "A new base of operations that doesn't have any traffic."

On the main floor, the tables continued in a single line under the *loggias* on two opposing sides. On the other two, a long bar faced the kitchen entrance and a waiters' station across the court. I could almost hear the buzz of ghostly conversations from years long past. Maya looped her arm through mine. Turning, I thought I saw her in a turquoise evening gown, her hair up and held in place by two mother-of-pearl combs of ancient design.

Cody found the staircase to the second level behind the bar, and we caught up with him. He focused his penlight on the treads. No one had climbed them in a long time. Bronze masks still hung on the wall next to us—comic and tragic faces. I was hearing the music in my mind; strings and woodwinds. From the second floor rail I looked down at the tables below. Through the cables of sixteen hanging chandeliers, supported from the ceiling grid, I thought I could see the blur of diners, waiters, dinner jackets and evening gowns as they moved about, cocktails in hand, drifting among the tables. The brittle flash and angular glitter of diamonds. The distant buzz of laughter, the clinking of fine crystal glassware. Altogether it shaped the look and feel and taste of a time gone by—now no more than a dusty memory. Now no more than a house full of artifacts.

I wanted to paint it; I could see the oily pigments moving, sliding around at the end of my brush, piling up in ridges that would slowly harden into what was called 'brushwork.' This was what Glass would never understand, what he disdainfully called 'the painter's eye.' There would be a feathery mixing at the edges, where the colors met and merged. I could *feel* it with the same immediacy as the impact of Maya's elbow in the center of my back at that same moment. I turned to discover her in her working outfit, close-fitting jeans, a pale blue work shirt with flap pockets over her breasts, and an automatic pistol in her waistband.

"The stairway to the upper level is over there. I don't know what you're seeing down here, Paul, but up above us is where it's going to happen tonight."

Méxican women are the ultimate realists. Maya was true to type in this regard, although she differed greatly from the norm in other ways. I thought she even relished her down-to-earth attitude. She knew I saw things differently from other people. There were some times when it was more appropriate than others.

When this mansion was used as a home, the second floor had consisted of bedrooms, dressing rooms, intimate parlors where the family retreated in informal dress. Probably a smoking room, library, or billiard room for the master of the house was an important part of the layout. I can say this not because I was ever a guest there or anywhere like it, but because I know the Méxican patterns. At the back were the staff quarters, and, in the corner adjacent to the Almeida mansion, flanked by four tiny windowless bedrooms that must have been unrelentingly steamy in the Guadalajara summer, was a narrow service stairway to the third floor. Cody, who had not heard the music and laughter, the tinkle of champagne flutes below, led the way. It was the path into danger he had walked many times before. As he started on the first step, I saw him reach to his belt and adjust his waiting revolver. His was a different reality from mine, grittier and more practical, with a wariness that came from being shot three or four times in the past. That was the reason why our partnership worked as well as it did. His well-tuned caution was also why we were all still alive.

Maya and I checked our guns. There is the past and there is the present. At the moment, I was more into nostalgia, which, in view of our task, suddenly felt right—we were going to defend the Church's investment in a longstanding fake. Our job was to prevent the reality of the present from intruding on its venerable, if bogus, history. What was more nostalgic than that? Even if you believe the past, if you embrace history, you still must take it with a grain of salt. It's usually narrated by people who weren't there to witness it, and when they were, they often have an ax to grind, just as we do, in viewing it.

Angling his penlight over the handle and the keyhole on the roof-level door, I watched Cody shaking his head. He turned back to Maya. I still had Natty's cardboard tube under my arm, an optimistic gesture, probably naïve, but if we did recover the Virgin, I wasn't going to simply roll it up under my arm.

"Sorry, but I'll do this as quietly as I can. My picks weren't made for a two-bit Méxican screen door lock that's been rusted shut for thirty years. They were great in Peoria, and they've been pretty good here until now." He placed his heel at the lock level and grunted softly as he pushed.

When it failed and gave way, the sound was more than I was hoping for, but, still, we weren't met by machine gun fire from the other side. Out on the roof we found it about four shades brighter under the moon. Below, we'd been looking through the glass covering on the courtyard that had a generation of airborne grit sifted over it. Now we were in position, not that we knew what that meant.

We found ourselves in a room with four glass sides, and ornate cast iron piers at the corners to support the glazed roof. To me, it looked like a garden shed from a time when the mansion roof had been a functioning *jardín* for the residents. This room would have housed tools and seedbeds, hoses and fertilizer bags. The floor below must have had a more formal staircase on the other side that we hadn't seen, because the family would surely not have been coming up to the roof this way. Later, this garden shed, with its translucent roof, would have furnished a place to raise culinary herbs at most for the restaurant years. Now it was mainly a storage place for empty pots and rotting hoses. Nonetheless, it was our launch pad for whatever was coming next.

"This is the endgame," said Maya, softly. Always on the hunt for English vernacular, it was a word she had recently learned. I could see her lips pressed tightly together.

"Going up against the connoisseur," I said,

looking at her.

"I still like him," she said.

Through the glass facing Almeida's mansion, we looked down a full story to the roof of what must have been his service wing. Without a ladder, there was no way to get down to it. I suspected it was occupied and our landing on the roof would be the cause for an alarm. When we came in before through the garage entrance opposite, this part of the complex had been screened by high plantings.

Looking toward the street in front, the tower room on the near corner of Almeida's house was at least forty feet away. The small garden we'd noticed earlier occupied the grilled space fronting Avenida Independencia, and at the back of it was our only hope—the chapel. We went out for a closer look. Below us, the roof was high and pitched on both sides to a tall ridge, like any cathedral in Europe, although it was a small building. The cruciform footprint was clear, and at the right arm of the cross, the roof peak came within inches of the building we stood on.

It was finished in copper roofing, the kind with vertical panels clinched together in ribs about a foot apart. The ridge was a little more than three feet below *The Opera* common wall, where we stood.

"This is doable," said Cody. As operations manager, he was obliged to take an optimistic tone here. "There'll be a tricky moment while we're standing on it, turning around with one hand on this wall, and bending over to slide down."

"I can do it," said Maya, without hesitation.

"I'm sure you can, but I'll need to go first," he said. "If it holds me, it'll hold both of you."

Perhaps it was the years-long silence of the voices

from the restaurant that had led Vidal Almeida to underestimate the potential risk of invasion from that quarter. Or maybe it was his armed guards. I assumed they were on duty twenty-four hours a day. Or it could have been his conviction that no matter what he did, God was on his side.

"One more thing, though," I said in a whisper. "We may be going in this way, but we won't be leaving this way."

"We will be leaving by the front door," Cody answered in the same muffled tone, "with our heads held high." I didn't know whether this was bravado, or that he actually had some plan he hadn't disclosed. Keeping it secret at this point was not a good strategy, I thought. I concluded he was winging it. With no further comment, he straddled the parapet and dropped silently over the side. He paused a second with his hands on our wall until he felt steady, then slid on his knees down the copper roof to the gutter, gripping the ridges with both hands to retard his pace. When he stopped, I dropped the tube down to him. Catching it with one hand, he set it in the gutter out of the way.

Maya went next. She had no trouble on the roof ridge, and when she slid down the slope with what I thought was remarkable control, Cody caught her securely by the butt with both hands to stop her from going over the edge. He was always concerned for her safety more than everything else. Maya turned and gave him a knowing look. A moment later we were all standing on the gutter. Fortunately, it was set into a trough in the stone on the top of the wall. That made it invisible from below, but also gave it the support to carry our weight.

We paused for a moment, listening for a response to our arrival.

The night was deadly quiet. From somewhere came the scent of jasmine.

From where we were, we could only be seen from the closest tower room at the street. I didn't think it was in use. The windows were covered with an opaque fabric on the inside.

The moonlight was strong enough for us to get around with no problem, but it also made us visible. The outer corners of the chapel walls below on the main level were marked by large squared stones. Deeply cut grooves between them divided the layers. In the U.S. these are called quoins. I suddenly knew what we had to do, and it looked a little chancy. We needed to stick our fingers and toes into these separations in order to reach ground level. They were about a foot apart. Here, Cody's weight would act against him. None of us had seen any of the *Spiderman* movies. It now seemed like that would have been a good idea.

"Here goes my manicure," said Maya, "all for another Boy Scout job. For the Church, even."

"You're going to heaven," I said, "whether you want to or not."

If we were hanging by our hands from the gutter level, it would be about seven feet more from our shoes to the ground. Not so terrible. If our fingers held, and we got decent support from our toes, enough to get even halfway down, a shorter drop would easily be manageable.

"What do think, big fella?" I whispered. "Maya and I can go down first and break your fall if your fingers give out."

"I could even catch *your* butt, then," Maya said to him, "now that I know exactly how it's done."

"I think I'll go first," Cody said, without further comment. From the firm set to his lips and jaw, he wasn't relishing this part of it. Neither was I.

He swung his legs over the edge, then turned and dropped down to his elbows. His toes must have found a grip because his body came away from the gutter and dropped a foot or so more.

"I'm good so far," he said softly, but I could still hear relief in his voice. One hand left the edge, then the other, and his head dropped out of sight. "Still good here and holding."

A muffled grunt suddenly came from below and I looked over to see Cody hit the ground, landing on both feet, but off balance, and sitting down hard. He shook his head and held his arms out from his sides, testing his shoulders. After a moment he turned from side to side and held his thumb up.

"Be sure you wipe the dirt out of the grooves before you put any weight on them," he said in a stage whisper.

We waited again before joining him, wondering if the impact of Cody's mass on the ground had caused a tremor, but nothing more happened. I'm sure that Maya and I both had finger strength greater than Cody's relative to our mass. Our toes were also smaller. And besides, we swept the dirt out of the grooves before we descended.

"How handy to find ourselves here at the chapel," said Cody, brushing himself off. "I bet I'm going to have a big bruise. Not that anyone would ever see it."

To my surprise, the chapel, which we entered

through the left side near the sacristy, as we had before, wasn't locked. Most likely the front wasn't either. Had we been wrong about Almeida having the Virgin? It didn't seem like he felt much at risk if he did.

"You know it's not going to be here," said Maya as we walked in. "We're Boy Scouts for nothing."

Cody flashed his penlight discreetly around the sacristy. Nothing was changed. In the chapel itself the only difference we found was eight frames of scaffolding leaning against one wall, ready for assembly near the altar, and my three devotional paintings already hanging on the front wall. The area above the altar was still blank and waiting.

"This makes sense," I said.

Maya made a subtle noise that suggested if I could make sense of this, then I could rationalize anything.

"How would it?" said Cody, in an irritated tone. "Do we want to be running around this place opening every damn door trying to find the Virgin?"

"Look, they just got hold of it tonight, right? They're not going to be hanging it the same way it was in México City. It must have been in some kind of special travel case on the road, so that won't be appropriate. A guy with this kind of collection is going to have his own framing shop somewhere around here. He's got things among his holdings he doesn't want outside framers to see. That's where we look next. Do you think he ever told anyone that the Raphael I did for him wasn't the real deal? And he had the frame ready for it when it came."

"How about those frosted glass panels in the garden walk you pointed out?" said Maya. "He wouldn't have a shop inside the house, or in the staff quarters. He wouldn't want them to know what's going on. But if it's underground, like near the archive you think he's got, wouldn't that work? That would be the right place for it."

Behind the chapel, a crescent-shaped landscaped terrace, echoing the outer curve of the sanctuary, made a transition to the service quarters, with two stone benches and a flight of steps descending toward the grand garden on the left. We moved single-file down to the lower level, holding to a line of trees that screened the staff quarters from the rest of the garden. It also provided a long band of shade from the afternoon sun. We paused about half-way from the back wall.

"I'm thinking that the security is mainly at the front entry, and at the garage where we came in before," whispered Cody. "They're not focused on the idea that anyone would come over the wall and be already inside."

"But remember the dog," I said. This might have been a Sheila Roper insight.

"He was calm when we came in," said Maya. "I'll let him lick me, if he wants to."

I made no comment on this.

Across the garden, farther down on the opposite wall, I could see a small light glowing within the inner gate at the garage. From what I could see, no one moved about inside. The light limestone color of the mansion walls around us was clear under the moonlight. The arches of the loggia above us were all distinct. Far on the right, near the corner below it, I saw the darker profile of a door at the garage level, but past the rusted entry doors, and their grilled gate, where the cars would have been parked inside.

"Let's check out that door at the back corner," I

said. "I don't think it leads into the garage, and we saw stairs going up when we were parked in there.

We followed the ghostly line of manicured trees and hedges to the back of the garden, and slipped along between the back wall and the boxwood hedge, which came only to waist level. I saw no sign of the dog, and I knew that he'd see us before we saw him, if he was out. At the far end, the glass panels began alternating with stone at our feet. We stopped behind one of the four tall sculptures at the fountain corners and scanned the garden, but nothing was moving. Twenty feet farther on we paused at the door. Back at the grand terrace, no lights were on and nothing moved.

Shielding it from the garage entrance gate with my body, I held the penlight on the lock as Cody went to work. Maya waited with her arms folded.

"This lock's much better kept than the one next door," he said a moment later, as he extracted his pick and pushed the door open. "I think this one gets some traffic."

CHAPTER 20
NATTY BOLLANDER

When his cell phone rang, Natty had been sitting on the loveseat in his room with his hands gripping his knees for some time. The lights weren't on, and the darkness was both soothing and comforting. He let it ring again. He was not used to confrontation. Although she'd gone off the deep end recently, Chiara had never before challenged him, and his life had been organized into long segments of solitude as he worked, mixed with low-key social evenings on the piazzas with Chiara. Most of the other friends he knew were people he'd met through her. He actively avoided other painters, people he might normally be expected to spend time with, because they would naturally want to talk painting. Having never explored much of the subject, Natty never did.

Knowing who it had to be, he finally answered the phone.

"Hey Natty! Sorry if I got you up. Everything went well—not a single hitch. What fools they all are! We're wrapping up here before we leave town. I'd like to be on the road before dawn, but I want to come by now and pick up that print you worked from. It's got my name on it, or at least Glassworks, on the tube. I'd just feel better if it wasn't kicking around here, and I know you're not going to want to take it back to Italy with you. We don't want to give people any ideas, do we? I thought..."

Glass's phone started crackling and popping as if he were driving through a minefield of electrical interference. Natty flew into a panic when he suddenly recalled that one of the armed thugs who broke in on him—they had never even had the decency to tell him their names—had taken that tube with him when he walked out the door.

"But, Dr. Glass, I don't actually..." Glass, whose sentences were being randomly parsed into syllables and single letters, finished with a cheerful, but incoherent, farewell tone and hung up. In contrast, the dial tone that followed on Natty's phone was perfectly coherent.

But Natty Bollander himself was not. He sputtered obscenities as he threw his belongings randomly into the suitcase. Checking his tickets and passport, he wasn't surprised to see he still had Chiara's too. It didn't matter now. That bitch could get back to Italy whatever way she could. He threw the paintbrushes into the wastebasket, tossed his toiletries loose into the suitcase along with an extra pair of shoes, and slammed the lid shut with a grunt.

Ten seconds later he was downstairs at the reception desk, tapping his fingers nervously as he rang the bell with the other hand. Five minutes later the night clerk, with sleep in her eyes, emerged from somewhere in back. Her hair was a mess and she wore a loose-fitting blue dress she had probably just pulled over her head.

"I'm checking out. I have a cab waiting. Please hurry!" He passed her his credit card.

Of course Natty had no cab waiting. He'd only said that to rush her. In a sudden flash of sanity, he pulled

Chiara's passport and air ticket out of his document case and slapped them on the counter. It was his way of being free of her for good. Now she'd have no reason to be coming after him. The girl he was looking at had no way to know this, but so what? He would leave a certain amount of chaos in his wake.

Most Méxicans, while courteous, are not inclined to rush, especially when prodded by a large panicky gringo with no manners. By glancing at the security camera monitor next to her computer, the night clerk already knew there was no cab waiting. The only one she ever called under conditions like this was her boyfriend, and he was waiting for her return in bed in the room behind.

"Was everything alright, sir?" she said in Spanish. She had also decided to speak no English to him, although she'd lived in Arizona for nine years as a child and spoke it perfectly.

"Let's wrap this up," Natty said, not understanding what she'd said. It wasn't like México was a first-world country—they were used to sorting things out after important people left. Dancing his fingernails along the hardwood countertop, he glanced back toward the entry. The girl pulled out a file and began leafing through some papers. Sitting at the computer, she pulled up his records and printed them out.

"You won't be joining us for breakfast this morning, sir? Because we have the waffle bar today." He understood *waffle* and *bar*, but the rest was lost on him. She managed a coy smile that some would have found borderline seductive. If Natty had been at all rational he would have seen how much she was enjoying this.

"Just hurry it up, OK? Jesus Christ. What in God's name does it take to get out of this dump?" He was disgusted with himself for the way he was acting, but it was OK, since she'd probably think he was an American. With a neutral look, she passed him the receipt, and he jammed it into his shirt pocket as he ran for the door. He heard it buzz open as he grabbed twice at the handle. Outside on the narrow apron, he saw no one on the street, but realized he'd left his suitcase at the desk. He whirled back inside to seize it before the door latched, and panting, careened back outside, clutching it to his breast.

On the apron, he was nearly hit by a white Ford van driven by Collin Welch, as it glided to a stop. Dr. Glass gave him a friendly wave from the passenger window, as if this meeting had been arranged. Natty's stomach contracted into a knot, and he nearly retched on the pavement. Glass waved him closer. His mouth held its toothy grin, but his eyes were deeply serious.

"You weren't leaving, I think, Natty? Don't we still have some business? The final detail we spoke of on the phone just a moment or two ago? It's no problem—give me the mailing tube now and Collin and I will be on the road. I assume it's in your suitcase?"

Foolishly, Natty had prepared no response to this inevitable question, thinking he'd be gone and would never have to hear it, at least not face to face like this. Collin Welch opened the driver's door and came over to him, placing a hand firmly on his shoulder. Natty couldn't look at his face.

"You make no move to pull it out," said Glass after a moment in a firmer tone. "Gestures, even by their absence, can be eloquent. This one goes even beyond that.

You are scaring me now, Natty, and I don't scare easily. Where's the tube?"

"Ah, I'm afraid I lost it." Natty tried to smile as if this were of no importance, given all the spectacular things he had done for Dr. Glass. "Probably the maid threw it away, because when I packed, it wasn't there anymore. Does it really matter that much? I mean, aren't we finished here?"

Natty was so intent on trying to assess Glass's response to this hopeful question that he didn't see Welch's fist airborne on a trajectory that ended at his abdomen, in fact, some inches in. Completely unprepared, he doubled over and fell to his face on the pavement, gasping for air.

"Don't injure his hands," said Glass quietly.

"He won't be able to talk for a while now," said Welch, who was no stranger to this move.

"I don't think the man had anything else to say. Check his bag, just in case."

Welch bent over under the streetlight and zipped open Natty's suitcase, throwing things out by the handful. Toothbrushes and underwear fluttered into the street. The laptop sailed over the pavement like a rectangular Frisbee, where it shattered corner-first against the opposite wall, the lid flying off onto the sidewalk. A pair of clean socks, rolled into a ball, landed next to it. Two paperbacks fluttered through the air like panicked pigeons. Welch shook his head and shrugged as he climbed back into the van and drove away.

After a few moments, the desk clerk came outside. Dawn was still two hours distant. Natty was clawing the pavement like an injured insect heading for cover, still breathing as if he'd been under water for a long time. The texture of the irregular paving stones was imprinted on his cheek. He didn't know she was there.

The girl squatted with her knees by his face. "Do you want me to get help for you?" she said in English. "I could call an ambulance."

Natty still couldn't speak, but he shook his head. He couldn't see her expression. The girl took his hand, the one that wasn't pressed to his abdomen. "I hope you don't think this is a tough neighborhood. We never have any trouble here. I don't understand how this happened. Did you know them?" She pressed her cool palm to his forehead, then to his neck, where his pulse was still surging. With a grunt, Natty rolled over on his back and looked up at her.

"Thank you," he managed to say, still wheezing. "I'm sorry." He gasped again and started coughing violently, doubling over.

"Are you bleeding?"

When Natty didn't answer, the girl stayed close by his side for a while with her arms wrapped around her knees in the chill morning. Finally he thought he would try to get up. She supported him as they went through the door. He waved off any thought of his luggage. Most of his things had already been run over several times by the early beginnings of traffic. He had seen that his laptop was a hopeless scattering of parts across the street. Inside, Natty leaned against the reception desk, grasping the edge. His breathing was better. She gave him back the key to the room he'd vacated twenty minutes before.

"My name is Lisa Moreno, Señor Bollander. You can stay up there until you feel better. We don't have anyone coming in for it. Do you need help going upstairs?

Natty nodded, perhaps seeing her clearly for the first time. His hazel eyes lingered on her face. "Yes, I do, Lisa." He realized he couldn't remember when he'd last had any real help. Chiara had often been fun, but rarely helpful. Lisa came around to the front of the desk and, in a businesslike way, pulled his arm over her shoulders as they started up the stairs, one at a time. They paused twice while he recovered his breath. At her healing touch, Natty felt he'd recovered a morsel of his humanity as well.

CHAPTER 21

I closed the door silently behind us, hearing it latch with the tiniest of sounds, as Cody led the way down a wide flight of stairs, moving the penlight from side to side. At the bottom, we were in a corridor that led only left, the direction of the garage entrance on the level above. In contrast to the sophisticated French décor of the upper levels, the style here was contemporary and utilitarian. Smooth walls were painted white, with a ceiling about ten feet high, and from the pale greenish moonlit glow at regular intervals over our heads, it followed the line of frosted glass panels along the Cruz Verde wing of the mansion. On the right, wide doors interrupted the wall at regular intervals. The first one in the series had a label that read, SIGLO XVIII, *Papel.* Eighteenth century paper art. I assumed these were engravings and drawings in a climate-controlled storage system. We passed two rooms marked for textiles, which surprised me. Maybe Almeida was a student of the art, although I hadn't seen any examples upstairs.

The fifth room, with a pair of doors, was labeled *MARCOS*, frames.

"Bingo," said Maya. The lock was contemporary and impressive, but it was an American brand that Cody had worked with often in the past. He had it open in less than two minutes. I secured the door behind us as Maya found the light switch.

The shop had a familiar look. In college I'd worked part time as a cabinetmaker's assistant, and I knew most of the tools. I saw a high-end miter saw, and two sets of adjustable clamping jigs that would draw a frame together from all four sides at once, and keep it square as the glue dried. Against the back wall stood a four-tier wood rack with stacks of interesting timbers and planks in different woods. As pressured as we were, the sight of it still made me want to linger.

The focus of the room's activity was a picture frame already hanging empty on the wall. Overall it was about six feet high by three and a half wide. I could only call the style high Baroque. The frame members meandered in width from eight to as wide as sixteen inches, and the outer edge incorporated a series of shields, arabesques, wings, acanthus leaves, and twenty other elements I didn't know the names of. The recessed parts were ebony, and all the overlaying elements were gold leaf. It was brilliant, and I could almost hear all of our jaws dropping. My vocabulary was exhausted just looking at it.

"You know that frame will totally overpower the Virgin picture," I said.

"Don't you think?" Cody said. "What could stand up to that? Not even my LeRoy Neiman." Maya was stunned into silence. She may have been imagining one of my portraits of her in it.

"I guess the point is the presentation," I said. "If the frame is this great, how much greater must the picture be? It prompts you what to think about it. You can infer what you're not actually seeing in front of you."

"It's simply divine," Maya said, excluding any trace of cynicism from her voice. I knew she wasn't thinking at all about the Virgin picture, only the frame.

Slowly, a prickly sensation was building on my skin. It felt like a sense of impending revelation, although I wasn't much of a believer in relics like the Virgin of Guadalupe. It put me in mind of all those pieces of the true cross that surfaced now and then. By this time, there were probably enough of them around to reconstruct Noah's ark. They all seemed top heavy with faith, but misty and vague on detail. Often the faith had a coerced quality that undercut its charm. Sometimes the choice had been believe it or be burned at the stake.

On one of the four worktables in the room lay a flat steel case of the right size. We gathered around it and I set the tube down at the end of the table. I had no intention of taking the case away with us. Cody lifted off the lid, which was not secured, and peeled back two layers of protective covering. Maya gasped. Even though she was not a believer, she was still Méxican. There was no doubt this was the Virgin of Guadalupe. The small hairs on the back of my neck stood up. I began to feel we'd really done something outrageous this time, not that Glass and Almeida hadn't, but the onus of doing this right was clearly on us.

The work light directly above showed a devotional picture in a style that looked to me like seventeenth, rather than sixteenth century, but I'm no expert. I studied it carefully. It was not like any of the three devotional works of mine now hanging upstairs in the chapel. The style of this painting was more like a folk effort, unsophisticated, without being downright crude. I suspected the painter had learned his craft from a neighborhood master, or in the atelier of a local painter of no great reputation. He had been a craftsman. There was nothing wrong with that—I considered myself a craftsman too. I'd always emphasized skill over inspiration, workmanship over genius. Results over pretense. Unlike many artists of the seventies and eighties, I made my own pictures because I had taken the trouble to learn the skills. Still, the longer I looked at it, the more the painting I was seeing left me strangely unmoved. I did not believe the legend that said it had first appeared in 1531 in the parlor of the Bishop of México City.

Cody and Maya were both staring at it in silence, shuffling their feet slightly as if unsure how to react. They looked at each other before they looked at me.

Profoundly aware of the moment, I bent over the surface, focusing on the detail. It was surely painted with oils, not some divine substance that defied definition. I could see the subtle brush marks, but there was no bravura stroke on this surface. The painter had made no attempt at artistic statement or personal flair. This was consistent with early Church art. At the edges, the primer, the pale under-painting that formed the first layer to seal the fabric, looked oddly recent to me; not as if it was painted yesterday, but not from the Renaissance or Baroque era, either. It had, overall, a disturbing freshness to it.

"I don't think this piece is nearly 500 years old," I said, keeping my voice low over the table. "Even 400 would be a long stretch." I shook my head slowly, feeling increasingly out of my depth. "I also don't think I understand what I'm looking at. This is more than upsetting, somehow. I feel let down by it."

"We should probably wrap this up and go, then," said Cody, always the realist. "Whatever this is, it's going to take some effort to get it out of here, and I'm ready to do it now before my butt stiffens up any more from sitting down hard like that."

Maya was nodding vigorously. "Once we're outside, we can decide how to switch it back with the one in the cathedral. This is no place for planning. I'm breathing too hard to think clearly."

But, for a moment, no one moved. The silence was suddenly tense. I began to wish I'd brought a pair of archival gloves, but I hadn't thought of it. Maybe I hadn't believed I'd be standing next to the Virgin picture at this moment, getting ready to stuff it into a not-so-sacred cardboard tube. I lifted the upper edge of the image, surprised to find the texture was familiar to my fingertips. As I began to roll it forward to fit the diameter of the tube, I stopped and bent over to examine the back. The linen, for it clearly was linen, and not some local maguey fiber that would have deteriorated into dust hundreds of years ago, had a look I knew disturbingly well.

It stopped me cold because it had been made on a *power* loom. The threads of the warp and weft were even and uniform, the spacing utterly consistent. It possessed nothing of the irregularity of old, handspun linen yarn, none of the inconsistent tension of a hand-thrown beater against the weft. I froze, unable to go on. This simply could not be, and I felt deeply confused. I tried to recall when power looms came in. Was it first around the last of the eighteenth century, when so many things were being mechanized with waterpower? I had handled old paintings done on European linen, and it seemed like the fabric was always hand woven until around the middle of the nineteenth century. My fingers released the image and it settled back nearly flat.

"What's wrong with you?" whispered Maya in alarm. "Are you alright? Paul, let's take it and *go*, *now*! We don't have a lot of time anymore. They'll be coming again soon!"

It was a moment or two before I could answer.

"It's a fake." I was almost stuttering.

"But we always knew it was a fake," she whispered, putting her hand on my arm and shaking it, as if waking me from some childish dream. "The Church just assembled the legend around an old picture, and then they fanned the flames under it for 400 years."

"No, no, it's not that way. This is *really* a fake; it isn't even that old. The canvas is machine made, so it can't have been made before 1850 or 1860. It might not even be as old as I am. I can't tell any closer than that." Even as a whisper, my voice was hoarse.

"Then the answer is obvious," said Cody. "This picture's been stolen and substituted before, just like it was tonight. This is no more genuine or important than Natty Bollander's copy that's now over at the cathedral treasury."

"Jesus." Feeling like I'd been struck in the face, I backed away from the painting with my hands in the air, appalled that I, the skeptic, had given it so much more credit than it deserved. "I wonder if the Church realizes this?"

"Of course they do," whispered Maya, hoarsely. "It's the biggest money maker they have in the Americas.

They would be the absolute last people on earth to say anything to suggest it wasn't real. Let's get out of here."

Cody pulled the protective fabric layers back over the image and put the steel top back on it.

So that was the end of the Boy Scout solution to the theft of the Virgin; the hands on exercise of ethics out of the public view, where we were the only ones who knew how noble we'd been at a critical moment. None of it mattered at all anymore. As we started toward the door, I heard another door close some distance away, and by a person who was not trying to be as quiet as we were. It may have been the same entrance we came in through.

I switched off the light in the framing studio, fearing it might leak out beneath our door onto the floor in the corridor. I sincerely hoped the guard would not be trying all the doorknobs as he came our way. I didn't want to act like a common burglar, committing violence against his staff inside Almeida's house, but we'd still take the guard down if he came too close.

Within the frame shop, the sound of our breathing was hoarse and strained as he passed. Maybe it was only mine, but it made enough noise for all of us. I heard no footsteps until he reached our door, but he didn't slow, and then they faded quickly. I hoped it was no more than a routine walk-through that was part of his regular pattern at this hour.

"I didn't lock that door behind us when we came in," Cody whispered. "I never do, just in case we have to leave that way in a hurry."

It was difficult to assess what that meant to the security person who had just passed. If he'd checked it, did he think it was his own omission? And therefore, like the Church, would he not be mentioning anything about it? That had to be it, if he wasn't alarmed enough to follow up by checking all the doors on the corridor. In the darkness, a droplet of sweat rolled into my left eye socket.

"This is good," said Cody, listening at the door. "We can learn something here. If he comes back this way, where he's already checked things out, that will mean there's probably no exit at the other end. But if he doesn't, we wait a bit for him to go somewhere else circling his rounds, and we follow the way he went. If I'm not mistaken, the front door is up in that direction. That's our salvation."

"Our salvation at this point is also getting out alive and without being seen," Maya said.

Ten minutes later I stuck my head outside the door. The guard hadn't returned our way. The frosted glass panels in the corridor ceiling were no brighter than they had been when we came in. No one was in sight in either direction. We crept along the way the guard had gone, fully exposed. Fifty feet down I realized I'd left the tube behind, but it didn't matter now. It might prompt Almeida to reexamine his security system for leaks, but we were finished with him. I couldn't imagine that he spent much time in the frame shop anyway. It was possible no one would put much importance on the cardboard tube and the framers might simply put it in the trash barrel as being of no consequence. As indeed it was.

Slightly farther down, a staircase rose at a point I thought corresponded roughly to the location of the garage entrance above. At the top, the exit door was closed. It might have been the door I noticed next to the impressive staircase going up. We had parked right next to it. The corridor went on toward the grand terrace and we followed it.

"This is going well," said Maya in a stage whisper. "I'm starting to think we might get out of here alive." Hurrying silently along, we all had our guns out. I didn't care anymore how the doors were labeled, although if one had said, *exit to the street*, I probably would have noticed. The corridor came to an end and a staircase at the right ascended through three turns to the terrace level. I slowly swung open the door at the top and stood in the shadow of the doorway, seeing no one on the grand terrace. We all knew the floor plan. The upper edge of the interior walls was starting to glow slightly. It was already too much for our purposes.

Feeling more confident, I came out past the door, which had partly obscured my view of the front corner of the terrace on the left. In a small side chamber next to the stairwell—some service room, I imagined—a young man in the white coat and black slacks of a houseboy was embracing a young woman in an expensive-looking dressing gown. One of his hands was inside it at the level of her breasts. I froze in mid-step. They were looking into each other's eyes from inches away. If Vidal Almeida had seen this, his reaction would have been volcanic. I felt that if I moved another inch myself I'd draw the girl's attention. The boy's back was turned toward me. But then Maya bumped into me from behind, and I lost my balance, lurching forward into a chair at a circular table set for breakfast. When the girl opened her dreamy eyes, they froze on me, and she screamed at the top of her lungs. The boy lurched backward out of sight, covering his ears with both hands. He crashed into some furniture out of view.

Cody burst through the doorway, gun drawn, and pulled Maya by the arm to one side. I regained my balance and rushed after them the thirty-odd feet to the entry stairs at Avenida Independencia. The girl kept yelling, although with less intensity as we fled. None of us looked back. From somewhere nearby an alarm went off. We careened down the five steps and piled up against the entry doors. Maya and I turned to face the expected troops with our guns out, while Cody struggled with the latches to the deadbolts. Suddenly he yanked one door open, and we flew through onto the street. Now, I thought, it's only a case of whether they can outrun us to the van, or just shoot us in the back as we sprint. But a single step out, Cody stopped, whirled around and pulled the door shut again. Reaching back on his belt with a practiced gesture, he pulled out his handcuffs and slid them through the two entry door pulls, where he snapped one cuff into the other at the front with a satisfying click.

Almost immediately, the doors were yanked inward again, but only a couple of inches before the cuffs pulled tight and held them nearly closed. When two shots were fired through the slit at nothing more than the building across the street, we were already well on our way to the van.

Of course, it was not over, and I was surprised Maya hadn't announced that it was. She was usually way out ahead of the endpoint of our cases. I thought Almeida's people would still be coming at us from the garage entrance on the Cruz Verde side of his house. From the way we were parked, the only way to go was forward up Independencia past the front of the mansion. The traffic behind us coming off Niños Heroes was already thick, although it was barely dawn. We jumped into the van and I gunned it up to the corner of Cruz Verde. There I inched forward with two cars swerving around me, ignoring the struggle at the entry doors, and looked down toward the garage entrance, expecting to find the entry flying open and two or three white Suburbans sailing out with guns blazing at every window.

Instead, a blue Ford sedan was parked in physical contact with the pair of rusted steel doors, holding them tightly shut. Perplexed, the security camera above scanned it back and forth. It could have taken in no more than the car's roof. I swung to the right and down the street, slowing as we approached the car. Sheila Roper looked out the driver's window and gave me a shy, but knowing, smile. Cody gave her two thumbs up. If I had needed to characterize her expression, I would have said she'd found her medium. Although I couldn't see her clearly, the figure sitting next to her had to be Chiara.

"Timing is everything," Sheila said, with a broad smile. A silk turquoise scarf covered her neck, but nothing obscured her triumph.

"I swear that women are now the new men," said Cody from the passenger seat as I approached Calle Juarez at the next corner. "I like that Sheila's style." He'd made another gesture to her as we passed that I couldn't make out in detail while I accelerated down Cruz Verde. Four hours later, after retrieving our luggage, we arrived at San Miguel and home.

CHAPTER 22

I'm not going to get into Maya's excessively blunt rap about this case. It didn't help that the crime had a religious theme; in her mind, that was something closely akin to witchcraft or voodoo. Nor did it strengthen my position that we had collected hardly anything monetary from it, even for expenses. There was only the original $500 retainer from Clarissa Phelps at the Minneapolis Academy of Art, and the money Maya had lifted from Glass's wallet. We had saved no one's life, nor had we prevented any crime from occurring, of which there had been too many to count. We'd done a few of them ourselves.

We had failed to get Glass arrested for kidnapping Maya, or for ordering the death of the thief, Carlos Ortíz, who had removed the la Tour from the VRC show in San Miguel. The greatest religious treasure of México (bogus or not) had been looted from right under our noses. Although we could have taken the latest version with us, we chose not to. I could go on, but from a sense of sturdy self-interest, I won't.

At least Maya put off launching her diatribe until two days after we were safely at home in San Miguel. But just to convey the flavor of it, had it been an Internet search, it would have included key words such as boy scout, tenderfoot, pro bono, fortune-teller, bankruptcy, numbskull, psychic, and many others too numerous to list. Her command of American slang was such that she needed to look up none of these before she launched them. Worse, Cody was present for all of it as we sat out in our garden for a final debriefing. We had stayed away from Harry's this time out of fear that someone might overhear our conversation and double over with laughter. The other tables can seem rather close when you're yelling.

When Maya had finished, Cody did not rise to my defense. After all, his butt was still bruised from our chancy descent from the chapel roof, and he'd been in a more introspective mood since we got home. I thought he was feeling his age on this case, but I knew I couldn't mention that. He was nursing his second planter's punch. His new, late middle period Matisse was now hanging in his bedroom so as not to embarrass the LeRoy Neiman football print over the sofa in his condo. I was currently giving him a C+ for decorating.

"Yet," I said, rising to my own defense, in the stunned silence that followed Maya's analysis. "I don't think we're done with this case."

"Oh," here she chuckled as if I'd made a tasteless joke, which I've been known to do. "We're done," Maya said. "We are *so* done. Or do you have Sheila Roper stationed out there with some new insight?" Cody gave me a quick look that struck me to silence. I had run into him and Sheila together that morning, hand in hand, in the *jardín*. He had stepped aside and sworn me to secrecy out of her hearing, saying he was trying to figure out whether they might have a future, and until he knew, he didn't want Maya to hear about his new connection.

"Just ask Sheila herself," I had said to him. "I

think she would know better than you." Obviously there was the age difference between them, but single women outnumbered single men in San Miguel by ten to one. I'd always thought that Cody could come up with an interesting woman, if only he gave up on Maya.

"No, I don't have more from Sheila, but I've got this," I said to Maya. I pulled out the list Cody and I had gotten from Natty Bollander, and slid it over to her. Since it recorded all the fake pictures Natty had painted for Glass, it was also a list of most, or even all, of the pictures he had stolen from museums all over the world. I didn't know whether he had ever used anyone else as a copyist. Part of our task that evening was to decide how best to use the list to bust him. I was thinking of both the FBI and Interpol, if they could manage to work together. I had faxed a copy to Clarissa Phelps earlier in the day, recalling how she had placed some faith in us early on. Of course, her la Tour was prominent on Natty's list.

"Amazing," Maya said after a while. "There are some incredible things here. I wonder where all the money from their sale went?"

"That," said Cody, "is one way the cops will have of leveraging him once they bust him. If he gives up the buyers of the paintings, which we don't have a list of, and the location of the money, he may live to see the light of day once again."

"But what about the murder of Ortíz and the kidnapping of me?"

Cody shrugged. "Capital crimes, but they happened in México. I'm sure Glass is back in the States now, and they'll want to hold him for all the art theft once they pick him up. Delgado will never get custody of him."

"What about Natty?" said Maya.

"Nothing will happen to him, I think." That's also what I wanted to think. "Sure, you could get him for conspiracy and fraud, I suppose, but those things happened in Italy, mostly, and only in one instance in México. The police would have to prove that he knew how the copies were being used, and except in the case of the Virgin of Guadalupe, I don't know how they could. The authorities here would decline to prosecute him because the Church would never support the idea that the Virgin was stolen and copied. To say nothing of more than once."

"And what about you?"

I shrugged. I had the Méxican shrug down like a native now. Even the corners of my mouth turned downward perfectly when I did it. "Me? I wasn't hit or injured, and I didn't fall off a building. No one even came close to shooting me."

"But I think you took a hit, all the same," said Cody quietly. The police employed psychologists too.

"What? Financially? We can handle it. Or do you mean that creeping disillusionment with mankind that comes from always dealing with the dark side of humanity as we do? That erodes your personality over time from a glittering pixyish character with shimmering wings into a rabid curmudgeon?"

"Not what I meant, although I *have* noticed that trend in you. I was thinking more of that moment in the frame shop when you started to roll up the Virgin and paused to look for the first time at the back. There was a kind of breathless hush as you bent over it. I could see that Maya felt it too. When you straightened up again, the excitement had gone out of your eyes, and it was replaced by something dimmer, a disillusioned look. You had wanted to believe that picture was *something*. Not that it was from 1531, or that it was created by miraculous means without paint. Or that thirteen people were reflected in its eyes. You always knew none of that was true. But you still wanted it to be something *real*, if only that it was the object that had been the focus of so much veneration for centuries. So much appeal and longing and heartbreak for tens of millions of people who had a cause or a reason to believe." Cody was still the old psychologist, and it was not always comfortable for the people around him when he put on his lab coat.

"And hope," said Maya. "Don't forget that. More than anything, I think you wanted to see hope in that piece of canvas."

I couldn't speak for a moment because I knew they were right. I could never be a believer the way most people were in México, and usually I didn't miss it—yet there were times, like that moment in the frame shop, when I had felt its loss.

Finally I said, "But that's how I look at every piece of canvas. I look at all of them with hope. That's why I'm a painter. Without that, you're only…a copyist."

That was true too, although I could see that neither of them was satisfied with my response. I wasn't either. It was more quick than honest.

We got onto lighter things then, like, where had we hung our Matisse? In the kitchen, I said. Art dazzles the eye and lifts the heart in any room. Matisse, the free spirit, wouldn't have been offended to see it near the sink. I could see him bending over, scanning it through his monocle, trying to recall just when he'd painted it, recalling the brushstrokes.

By that time, we had handled as much of the heavy lifting as we could, or perhaps, as we wanted to, on this case. It was a relief, Maya said, that only two people had died; the burglar Carlos Ortíz, and the guy in the warehouse in Baker Falls that Cody had killed when he jumped out at us, leveling his gun. It was better that only one of them had been our doing. That was on the low side of average. It was acknowledged by all of us that too many loose ends remained, but you could never fix everything, we had proven that every time, and this case had truly been international in its scope. Even in the world of real cops and official justice, guilty people often walked away from what they had done. The copy list from Natty was our only remedy for this. I thought it still might work.

Then, when we were nicely relaxed, I heard the fax machine start up with its insistent whirring in the dining room as I was mixing another round in the kitchen. Don't ask why it's in the dining room—I guess it's easier to hear when we're out in the garden. There's a phone jack in one corner and there's no room for it in the kitchen. It takes a little bit of time while the machine spits the message out one line at a time, as if the content needed review by a third party, so I finished the drinks and served them in the loggia before I went in to retrieve the printout. We weren't expecting anything. Maybe it was our next case coming in. I thought our nearest conversation, once we'd put Bernhard Glass and his plots to bed, was going to be about when, or if, it might arrive.

When I bent over the machine, I saw that a faxed newspaper clipping had arrived from Clarissa Phelps. A handwritten note across the top read, "I won't ask whether this is your doing, even indirectly, because it's so crude. I can't imagine that it is, but somebody certainly caught up with him. You weren't the only one who had his number. We've taken down the la Tour once again. And thanks, Paul."

Art World Shaken by Murder of VRC Director.

Dr. Bernhard Glass, 59, for the past 12 years director of The Vergruen Reference Collection, was found hanged this morning in his Baker Falls, Texas office. Arriving at work at nine o'clock, his secretary discovered his body bound hand and foot, hanging from a hook in the ceiling that, according to her statement, hadn't been there the night before.

Although an investigation had recently begun over the discovery of several genuine old master paintings in a Méxican showing of the Vergruen collection, Glass himself was not under suspicion, and his death has been ruled a homicide. Police say they have no suspects at this time. The VRC, as it's familiarly called, is an educational institution that holds and exhibits the world's largest collection of counterfeit paintings. With an international reputation in the field of art forgeries, Dr. Glass was formerly chairman of the art department at the prestigious…

I felt the blood draining from my face. Two dead on this case had become three. I'd had a number of serious quarrels with Glass. I believed he was an obnoxious fake, worse than any in the VRC holdings, but I wouldn't have wished that end on him. I brought the report out to the others and sat down without comment, finishing my drink in a single draught.

"So the Méxican boy scouts get justice, after all," said Maya, passing it to Cody. After her kidnapping, she could find no mercy for Glass.

"He was playing a high stakes game. Tough, though, without a trial," said Cody, pushing the fax aside after he read it. All three of us sat there staring at the fax as if it had more to say, but it remained silent.

"I was the judge," I said, with no sense of justice or triumph. "And I was also the jury."

Cody nodded in agreement. "Yes, you were, although I wasn't going to bring that up."

"So, say it, then," said Maya.

Cody scratched his neck and made a grim face, then touched her hand before he began.

"It was the tube with Glassworks, care of Natty, as the address at general delivery in México City. Paul left it behind in the frame shop when we discovered we weren't taking the Virgin away with us. When Almeida saw it, he must have thought that he'd been duped by Glass. He still had the 'real' Virgin in his possession, but he didn't believe it anymore. I'm sure he'd already given Glass the money. Almeida could have brought in some canvas expert, have him look only at the back, and he'd know it was a fake. Glass was doomed, even though he'd delivered the Virgin from the cathedral in Guadalajara directly to Almeida. He did exactly what their deal called for. Unfortunately, he was tripped up by a fake, just like all the collectors who donated their mistakes to the VRC."

"And like so many other pictures in the VRC," I said, "if the Virgin ever appeared in their collection, no provenance would be listed. Just too embarrassing, in this case, for the Church." I didn't have much to add to this. I had never intended to set Glass up for his death. I'd always thought he'd be unreachable back in the States unless we could use Natty's list to persuade some people with real clout to go after him. After all, Maya was the only one who'd ever gotten that close to him before. I knew it wasn't likely to happen again. When I stood in the frame shop and realized that the Virgin was a recent fake, I was so upset that all I wanted to do was flee the scene. The cardboard tube was of so little importance at that point that I didn't even think of it until we were well down the corridor. I could remember speculating that Almeida might never hear about it. Glass was brought down by another unintended consequence—this time, one of mine. Usually they brought down the criminals, but I wasn't immune to the same effect.

To consider whether or not Almeida might have noticed on his own the same problem of a too-recent canvas on the Virgin picture would only be self-serving speculation on my part. I don't work too hard at letting myself off the hook. Lessons like this come to the surface in most of these cases, usually at great cost to someone. We were lucky that it has never been one of us, so far.

"Glass did fulfill his end of their deal," I said. "But the great connoisseur director of the VRC didn't know a fake when he saw it."

"And did you?" said Maya, coolly. "Mr. Boy Scout First Class? I know you can paint them, probably as well as Natty can."

I felt that because of Glass's death I'd been promoted from Tenderfoot, skipping over several grades, but not to the top.

"I don't know what kind of connoisseur of painting I am, but I always knew you were the real deal," I said. "I'm expert enough for that." Maya was never easy, which was one of the reasons I valued our connection so much.

"And what about Natty Bollander?" said Cody. "There's a loose end of major proportions. I'm sure this will really deep end him."

"I agree," I said. "But there's also the chance that this is his means of redemption. It could wake him from his deep sleep. If he can find it in the pain of losing his livelihood and his love at the same time, he might be able to do the one thing that could save him."

"He might finally begin to paint," said Maya.

"That's what always saves *me*," I said.

Visit the author's website at
www.sanmiguelallendebooks.com

www.ingramcontent.com/pod-product-compliance
Lightning Source LLC
LaVergne TN
LVHW091044080826
845145LV00002B/614

* 9 7 8 0 9 8 3 2 5 8 2 7 8 *